HATTIE MARSHALL
and the
Prowling Panther

HATTIE MARSHALL
and the
Prowling Panther

Debra Smith

CROSSWAY BOOKS • WHEATON, ILLINOIS
A DIVISION OF GOOD NEWS PUBLISHERS

Hattie Marshall and the Prowling Panther

Copyright © 1995 by Debra Smith

Published by Crossway Books
            a division of Good News Publishers
            1300 Crescent Street
            Wheaton, Illinois 60187

Cover illustration: Doug Knutson

Cover design: Cindy Kiple

First printing, 1995

Printed in the United States of America

Library of Congress Cataloging-in-Publication Data
Smith, Debra, 1955-
    Hattie Marshall and the prowling panther / Debra Smith.
        p.   cm.
    Summary: Hattie, a spunky twelve-year-old, frequently needs to call on the Lord's help as she experiences both the dangers and the fun of family life on a Texas farm in the 1890s.
    [1. Farm life—Texas—Fiction.   2. Family life—Texas—Fiction. 3. Christian life—Fiction.   4. Texas—Fiction.]   I. Title.   II. Series: Smith, Debra, 1955- Hattie Marshall frontier adventure series ; bk. 1.
PZ7.S644685Hat 1995   [Fic]—dc20   94-36498
ISBN 0-89107-831-2

03		02		01		00		99		98		97		96		95
15	14	13	12	11	10	9	8	7	6	5	4	3	2	1

For Mama and Papa Chambers

CONTENTS

❖

1

❖

Palmetto Pontoons

It seems like the minute you stop worrying is usually when you better start up again, Hattie thought, sticking her head out of the wagon. "The ferry is *what?*" she called.

"It's gone," said her brother Sam. "They must've moved it when the river rose and covered the dock."

Mama, Gramma, and Hattie ignored the steady drizzle and climbed down from the wagon. The flooded, rusty-colored river below them hardly resembled the drowsy, gray Sabine they had crossed last month. It was an unwelcome surprise.

"It started raining the day we got to Louisiana," said Mama. "I should've expected this and had us start home sooner."

"We had to stay as long as we did. Millie needed us," said Gramma. "It's not every day your sister has a baby."

Seems like every other day, thought Hattie, but she held her tongue. The first week with her five younger cousins had been fun, and the exciting

9

arrival of the sixth kept them busy. But as the rain kept coming, the house grew smaller and smaller. By the third week she was plumb weary of sleeping on a mat on the floor and washing other people's clothes. And she wasn't the only one who felt that way. When Mama finally said to pack up, Hattie had never seen a wagon loaded so fast.

"Maybe the ferry is tied nearby," said Sam. "I'll have a look."

The rest climbed back into the wagon, where Rosalie sat waiting.

"What'll we do if he can't find it?" she asked.

"Swim across," teased Hattie.

Her sister shivered. Rosalie was afraid of water; even though she was sixteen, she had never learned to swim. Though Hattie was four years younger and had only paddled around in the pond a bit, she was usually fearless about such things.

"We'll see," said Mama, opening a large basket. "Might as well eat while we wait."

They listened as the soft plopping of raindrops on the wagon's canvas top grew stronger. Their meal of salty ham and cold cornbread tasted soggy. A few minutes later the smacking sound of a horse's hooves stomping through mud told them Sam had returned. Four heads peeked out of the wagon.

"Did you find it?" they chorused.

He shook his head, slinging water from his black drover's hat. The long coat was as plastered with mud as his bay mare's coat. His lean, tanned face and blue-gray eyes were dark with concern. "Well, Mama, what do you want us to do?"

Hattie's mother stared across the flooded river to the Texas shore on the other side and rubbed her forehead.

"We can go back to Aunt Millie's and wait till the water goes down," said Rosalie. "The ferry might be back by then."

"No," groaned Hattie and her brother. "That could take *weeks*," Sam added.

"Besides, I can't imagine how your Papa has managed the place by himself this long," said Mama. "And the next crossing is even further than Millie's place. I don't know . . ."

Gramma spoke up. "You know, the first folks to settle here didn't have a ferry. Some built rafts, but others swam their teams and floated the wagons across. If the bottom's tight, a wagon's sort of like a boat. They'd tie palmetto branches to the sides to help it along."

Sam's ears perked up. "I've heard of that. Our load's not heavy—it should work."

Mama pondered a moment, then sighed. "All right . . . what else can we do? Girls, you help Sam fetch the palmetto while we get the wagon ready. Don't forget your coats and a knife."

When they were ready, Sam led his sisters to a low-lying wooded area. It was muddy but not flooded. Clumps of tall palmetto plants waved back and forth among the moss-laden trees.

"I'm not going in there," announced Rosalie.

"Mama told us all to help," Hattie reminded her.

"Then I'll help with the wagon." Rosalie spun on her dainty heel and retreated back up the road.

"Wait a minute!" yelled Hattie. "That's not fair! Sam, she'll do anything to keep her precious self from getting dirty."

"Don't worry about it," her brother said, already nearly up to his knees in mud. "We would have had to spend all our time getting her unstuck anyway. Watch out for snakes now."

Hattie shuddered as she waded into the mire. Water was one thing, but snakes . . . She'd already seen a man snakebit once.

"C'mon, you know they're more afraid of us than . . ."

". . . than we are of them. I know," she muttered. "I just don't want to scare any of 'em."

The tough stalks were hard to chop, and the sharp, green fans sliced into her fingers. But soon they had a large pile, which they dragged to the wagon, where Gramma was cutting long lengths of twine.

Rosalie peeked out and snickered. "You look like two pigs from the same wallow."

Hattie glanced down at their lanky forms coated with swamp bottom. As usual, Sam considered Rosalie beneath his notice and just went to work on the wagon.

"Hattie, look at your hands," said Gramma. "We

should've found you some gloves. Clean them up, then bring my salve."

"Yes'm," said Hattie, climbing into the wagon where Rosalie was packing away loose items so they wouldn't bounce out of the wagon during the float across the river.

"Get that nasty coat out of here, Hattie. You're dripping on everything."

"Oh?" Hattie slowly peeled off the long, gray coat, then, quicker than a squirrel's blink, deliberately tossed it right onto Rosalie!

"Ugh! What are you . . . You little wretch!" Rosalie shrieked.

"I just didn't want you to feel left out," Hattie cackled as she dove through the back flap of the wagon. The coat flew after her, landing on the road with a loud splat.

"Hattie, behave yourself," snapped Mama. "Don't we have enough trouble without you two squawking at each other?"

Hattie opened her mouth to say that she didn't start it, then noticed Sam shaking his head as he rubbed off a grin. It was nearly impossible for Mama to find fault with Rosalie. Hattie would just be wasting her breath.

Finally, after careful tying and retying, the wagon was ready. Sam made a final inspection, with Gramma on his heels. Hattie suspected that he enjoyed feeling responsible for the womenfolk. Now nineteen, he was as tall as Papa and was acting more like him every day.

It didn't occur to her to be nervous until Gramma insisted on having prayer before they began the crossing. Her strong, bony hand grasped Hattie's as they stood in a quiet circle.

"Dear Lord," said Gramma, "You know how bad we need to get home, and this appears the only way. Please take us safely through the waters just like You took the people of Israel through the Red Sea and on across the Jordan River. We know You'll help us, and we're much obliged. In Jesus' name, Amen."

Hattie suddenly realized she'd never seen either of the women in her family in water higher than their knees. She'd always assumed older folks just didn't care to be in the water. But now she wondered . . .

"Gramma, can you swim?" she asked hesitantly as she climbed back onto the wagon.

"No, honey," Gramma said quietly.

"Mama?"

Mama shook her head.

Hattie felt a hard knot begin growing in her stomach, and her voice got shrill. "Well, why didn't you ever learn?"

"Hattie, this ain't the time," Sam interrupted, handing her a long, sturdy pole. "Here. Sit next to Mama and hold this out between the mules. If one of them gets in trouble, stick it under the harness and lift up as hard as you can. I'll ride upstream and try to keep stuff from drifting into you all."

The two chocolate-colored mules were less than willing to wade into the floodwater, but Sam and Mama urged them on.

"Hi-ya! Come on, Droop. Let's go, Penny."

The old mule they called Droop stretched out his nose as if gauging the distance across the river. Then his long ears wilted, and he leaned back on his haunches.

"Uh-oh," said Hattie. She'd seen him do this to Papa before when the work had been hot and hard. Once Droop's ears went down, you might as well call it a day. Papa didn't like to whip animals, and he had a peculiar fondness for this old mule who'd been around longer than Rosalie. Instead Papa would coax him with a bucket of corn, or else unhitch the plow and let him sit there looking silly. Today they could do neither.

Soon everyone was clucking and hollering except Rosalie, who sat quietly. Sam found a whip in the wagon and popped it in the air. Penny jumped, but old Droop just held firm. Sam waded his mare out to tug at the mule's bridle.

"Come on, Droop. This ain't no time to play. Get up, now!"

Hattie pondered their dilemma. What they needed was a bucket of corn. Wait a minute . . . She scrambled to the back of the wagon and dug into the food basket—the cornbread!

"Sam," she called, "try this."

"Good idea," he said, catching two pieces of the

dry bread as he dismounted. Stepping ahead of the mule, he held out a slice.

Old Droop sniffed and stretched his neck. His long upper lip wiggled, barely touching the bread. Sam let him nibble, then moved away. Droop let out a bray that probably could be heard back home.

Sam grinned. "Yeah, I know you want more. But you'll have to come out here to get it."

Droop brayed again, long and mournful. Then he stood up and stretched toward Sam. Another step, a nibble . . . and before anybody could say a word, the stubborn mule was swimming!

The wagon lurched as if determined to stay in the soft mud, but there's a lot to be said for hungry mulepower, and soon the rig pulled free and started to float.

Hattie glanced back to see if the wagon bed was taking in any water. It was dry. Rosalie had planted herself in the middle, her strawberry-blonde curls afrizz and her eyes as wide as green saucers. Hattie had never seen her sister so scared. She wondered if Rosalie would bite her lip in two before they reached the other side.

Gramma stood behind the high wooden driver's seat, patting Hattie's shoulder now and then while carefully watching upstream. Mama, her mouth set in a white line, wouldn't take her eyes off the mules.

About thirty yards out, Hattie relaxed a bit. Sam's mare Chica swam steadily as he pushed floating limbs and brush out of their path with his pole.

This is really going to work, she thought. What a story they'd have to tell at home!

But when they reached the middle current, obviously faster and foamier than what they'd faced up to that point, Hattie could feel the river pulling them off course. Mama urged the mules on as they fought to keep from drifting downstream.

"Give 'em some rein!" called Sam. "They can't swim with . . ." He broke off, straining to keep a clump of brush from colliding with them. There was no telling what old Droop would do if something whacked him in the head.

Hattie held her breath. Sam's mare was swimming for all she was worth. Stretching out his pole, Sam shoved the brush pile. It veered off, barely missing the mules. Droop snorted and shook his head but kept swimming.

Hattie sighed and unclenched her hands long enough to wave at Sam. But he wasn't looking at her right then.

"Look out!" he cried, pointing upriver. A huge cypress trunk was drifting in the current and was headed right toward them.

It reached Sam first. He tried to deflect it with the pole, but the pole snapped in two as the log rolled into Chica, knocking her under the violent current.

Hattie screamed. She jumped up but could only watch helplessly as Sam and the mare floundered.

The log was coming at them fast. She tried to reach across Mama with her pole.

Gramma grabbed her skirt and yelled, "Sit down, Hattie!"

The warning came too late.

The log rammed them broadside, but incredibly, the wagon didn't break up. Instead it bounced and lunged, nearly turning over in the current. Hattie wasn't holding on to anything except the pole, and suddenly she felt herself flying back. She hit the water with a cold shock. Then the rushing river filled her nose and mouth and closed over her head. She kicked and swung her arms, grabbing wildly for the wagon. It was no use. Choked and blinded, the river swiftly pulled her away from the family she loved.

Sinking deeper, she realized that thrashing wildly was the worst thing she could do. Her chest ached as she tried to remember the swimstroke Sam had taught her. *Where was he? Please let him be all right. Was he in trouble in the river too?*

Slowly, somehow her arms and legs got into rhythm as she struggled to reach the surface. She couldn't believe the vast difference between the quiet pond back home and this muddy torrent. Her long skirt didn't help. Her lungs began to burn.

Lord, I don't want to die now.

She kicked harder and felt a cold blast of wind. She kicked again and came up gasping. Fighting to breathe, she strained to see through the dark mass of her hair. Her water-clogged ears didn't hear the warning cries, nor could she see the log tumbling toward her.

Colliding hard with her head and shoulders, like a mighty hand, it shoved her back under the water.

No! Hattie wanted to scream. *Not again.* She clutched desperately at a small branch, wrapped her arms around the log, and held on. It was her only hope.

2

❖

Downriver

The cold soaked through Hattie's weary muscles and right into her bones, numbing them as she kept clinging to the large log that was her lifeline. Had water ever been so cold or a day so long? How much longer could she hang on?

At least the rain had stopped, letting a feeble sun break through the clouds. Hattie raised her aching head and looked around. She saw only the river and the trees—with no sign of her family or any familiar scenery. She watched carefully in case the log drifted closer to shore. Some folks said the Sabine flowed all the way down to the Gulf of Mexico. She wondered what floating in saltwater would be like, but that was silly—she could never hold on that long anyway.

She shifted around, trying to get comfortable without relaxing her grip on the log so much that she'd fall off. She stared at her raw, numb fingers and marveled how they kept digging into the ragged bark without even being told to. *Amazing what a body can do when left to take care of itself*, she thought.

Take care of herself? That was a new experience for Hattie. Sam had always been there. If not, then Mama, Papa, or Gramma. Being the youngest meant someone always looked after you, even when you'd rather they didn't.

But where were they now—safe on the Texas side of the river, searching for her, going home for help? The memory of Sam and Chica struggling in the water tortured her. What if Sam . . . *He's a good swimmer*, she told herself. And if at all possible, Sam would never leave the river without her.

Near sundown she heard crackling noises over the drone of the river, like wood splitting. A logging crew?

Hattie looked wildly about. There was no one in sight. But the view ahead made her heart nearly jump out her chest—a logjam!

A bend in the river had created a natural dam. This was the best opportunity she could have hoped for. But she'd have to be careful; a person could easily be crushed in such a heaving pile of wood.

As her log drifted closer, she braced herself for the impact. When the log crashed into the dam, it bounced crazily. She hung on, praying it wouldn't roll and take her under the water or maybe even underneath the logjam, where she would surely drown.

At last the log bobbled slowly to a gentle rocking, and Hattie decided to try to stand on top of the logjam. Needles shot through her legs as the feeling returned. Carefully she stepped across to the next log. It held her weight.

The next log she stepped on began to sink, so she jumped quickly to the next one, a tree still covered with foliage. Grabbing small limbs, she cautiously made her way through—until she felt something smooth and soft against her skin.

She drew back her hand as a fat, brown moccasin snake slithered up the branch. Hattie tried to scream but found that her voice was gone. Instead she scrambled on across the woodpile, leaving bits of skirt and skin behind.

When she finally reached the bank, what a joy it was to dig her fingers into the slippery, red clay! Then, remembering the snake, she kept climbing. It took the last of her strength to reach the bluff overlooking the river. There she collapsed on the wet grass and stared at the sun slipping from sight.

"Dear Lord," she whispered, trying to sound like Gramma, "I don't know why You sent that log in the first place, but thanks for helping me hold on. Don't let Mama worry herself sick, and please . . ." Hattie clenched her mouth tight to stop its trembling. "Please let Sam be all right."

As the evening breeze grew colder, she began to shake all over. She realized that her clothes would take all the next day to dry. She had to find shelter before dark.

Nearby, a stand of loblolly pine whispered an invitation. Quickly she piled pine straw beneath one of the trees and propped fallen limbs against the trunk. It wasn't much of a lean-to, thought Hattie, but maybe it would at least break the wind.

She burrowed in. It was a warm, if prickly, bed for a sore, soggy creature. Soon she was asleep, paying no mind to the harsh grunt of a gator somewhere below or to the hoots of the noisy owls above.

A half-moon was resting on the horizon when a rifle crack split the early morning air. Hattie jerked awake, trying to remember where she was and why. Then she heard a familiar cry.

"Hat-tie-ee!"

She tried to yell back, but her swollen throat could barely squeak. She waited, straining to hear her name again.

Another call came, but it was fainter.

She jumped up, knocking over the lean-to. Grabbing one of the limbs, she struck it against the pine tree.

"Sam, I'm here!" she croaked. Frustrated tears rolled down her cheeks as she thrashed the limb harder and harder. "I'm over here."

He finally heard her and rode up the hill at top speed.

"Hattie? You all right?" he called, leaping off Chica.

A sob choked her as she stumbled toward him in the dark. Then suddenly she was wrapped in his strong arms. *Thank You, Lord*, was her only thought. *Thank You so much, for both of us.*

In the dim light she could see that Sam's face was as tear-streaked as her own. Only once, when his dog had been killed by a panther, had she ever seen her brother cry. His display of concern for her warmed her heart.

"I was so scared," she whispered. "I didn't know if you and Chica had . . ."

"We got separated. I swam to shore before discovering you'd fallen in. You were already nearly out of sight."

"Are the others okay?"

"Yeah . . . just in a frenzy. But I knew you'd hang on," he said hoarsely. "I just knew it."

Dawn broke with Hattie nestled beside a small, crackling fire. Her stomach was growling like a caged animal.

"Wish we had something to feed that critter," said Sam. Then he smiled. "Speaking of critters, you should've seen Mama heading the wagon home. Old Droop hasn't moved that fast in ten years."

Hattie nodded, not thinking about mules but about how close she'd come to never seeing her brother's smile again. It stretched across his tired face to reveal white, even teeth and enormous dimples; her own were puny by comparison. Combined with the warm, blue sparkle of his eyes, his smile could light up Hattie's whole day.

"Are you thawed out yet?" he asked.

She nodded again and tried to speak again. But it was no use; her voice just wasn't up to it.

"Well, this is one time I get the last word," he said, hoisting her onto Chica's saddle. "We'll ride upriver and hit the main road. Papa will surely be on the way, and that's our best chance to meet up with him."

Sure enough, by mid-morning a dozen riders topped the hill in front of them, red mud flying from the horses' hooves. Hattie was always pleased to see her father, but never more than today. Looking as though some unbearable load had been lifted from his broad shoulders, Papa swung her onto his saddle.

"Thank the Lord," he said, holding her tight as Sam told about their adventure. For a moment Papa rubbed the face that matched Sam's and her own, and his dark moustache quivered a little.

"We'd better get you home, girl," he said. "Your mama's worried sick."

With that they turned homeward. The neighbors who had roused before daylight for the grim task of searching the river were now in a jolly mood.

"Hattie, I'll bet your mama's fixing the prettiest pan of biscuits and redeye gravy you ever saw. How many could you put away right now?" asked Mr. McKinney, who owned the sawmill.

"As many as you," she croaked.

The large, red-bearded man chuckled and patted his stomach affectionately. "Then I hope she makes two batches."

"Pot o' coffee won't do no harm neither," added another.

Snuggled in her father's coat, Hattie glanced back at Sam riding with Mr. McKinney's son, Vince. They were close friends with much to catch up on. She smiled at Sam's chatter, glad he was free of the heavy burden of searching for her.

Her stomach growled again. She tried to tell Papa how long it had been since she'd eaten, but all she could do was cough.

He felt her hot cheek and urged the gelding to a gallop.

3

❖

Cabin Fever

Like Papa, home had never looked so good to Hattie. When they turned off the muddy logging road onto a narrow trail leading to the house, the women inside heard the hoofbeats. They rushed out like hens from a coop as the men shouted, "We found her!"

Mama reached Papa's horse before he could come to a stop, and the mud from the hooves splattered her apron. She didn't seem to care, snatching her girl down with a joyous cry. Gramma rushed up then, and Hattie thought she just might smother between them. The neighbors who had waited with the women through the long morning now waited their turn to squeeze the rescued girl as well.

As Hattie tried to answer their questions, the coughing started again, and Gramma hustled her inside. "This child's taking pneumonia, sure as the world. Rosalie, you start the water to boiling and stoke up the fire. The rest of you can feed those men out on the porch."

Hattie sat by the fire with her plate of biscuits as a steaming bath was prepared for her. Then she soaked for a long, long while, thankful to be warm and full again. Meanwhile, Gramma fixed herb tea for her to drink and mustard plaster to put on her skin. Hattie was so glad to be home, she didn't even mind the mustard plaster.

As the days passed, however, the pneumonia turned out to even be more trouble than expected. Gramma fussed and worried until Hattie's chest was blistered from the hot plasters. Hattie didn't want to see any more tea or onion soup. Still, Gramma insisted they were the best cures around, and no one disputed the point. Years before, when her folks lived near an Indian camp, the women had shown Gramma's mother how to use wild plants for medicines. So far the Marshall clan had never needed a doctor.

"This room is never going to smell right again," Rosalie grumbled one morning. She was dressing in the small bedroom she and Hattie shared, and from which she had been ousted the past three weeks. Gramma's hot breathing concoction of turpentine and pine needles sat on the trunk.

"At least you don't have to live in it," muttered Hattie. She watched Rosalie tie on a faded, yellow bonnet, then fumble with a pair of oversized gloves.

"I'd rather spend a month in bed than pick cotton. Look at these hands!" Despite the gloves, Rosalie's hands were cut and blistered.

As usual, Hattie was unsympathetic.

"Quit complaining. Pretty soon you'll be back in the kitchen and I'll get the blisters. Besides, it's a gorgeous day."

Rosalie "harrumphed" as she slammed the door leading onto the breezeway. Hattie stared out the window at the sun's first rays spilling across the yard. She would have enjoyed watching her persnickety sister pick cotton, but what really grieved her was that she was missing a most spectacular autumn. The rains had been followed by first frost, setting the forest ablaze with color. Though this part of Texas was called the Piney Woods, many hardwoods flourished as well. Hattie's favorite was a giant red oak that spread its crimson branches across the yard. Countless afternoons she had perched in a comfortable fork to read and watch the goings-on around the farm.

The bedroom door swung open as Mama balanced a tray of breakfast and her sewing basket. Hattie inhaled a muffin while giving the basket a dubious look. Her mother had tried to occupy her with quilting the week before.

"It's good to see you have an appetite," said Mama. "Look what I found."

She held up a white cloth clamped to a round, wooden hoop. It was the sampler Hattie had begun when she was eight. Erratic purple lines suggested the letters of her name, which was all she had finished. Hattie hated sewing. No matter which finger she wore the thimble on, another got stuck; and no two of her stitches were ever the same. She moaned and rolled her eyes.

"Mama, I don't *feel* like sewing."

Her mother sat on the bed, quiet exasperation written on her soft, round face. Except for the lines etching the fair skin, it was just like Rosalie's. Her hair used to be the same too, though it had faded to a peach color with silver strands that laced her tight bun. Mama complained about that, but actually Hattie thought her hair was pretty.

"Honey, it's important to know how to sew. Someday you'll need to make clothes for your family. I might not be around to show you then."

"Sure you will. But I'd rather buy them from the catalog anyway."

"That's for folks with lots of money, which you can't count on. The point is, I'm not being mean teaching what you need to know." She paused. "You don't fuss about schoolwork . . ."

"You say an education's important."

"All right, then, think of homemaking as part of your education." She stood to go. "Your first assignment is to work on this when you finish eating."

"Then can I go outside?"

Mama shook her head. "Too chilly. We don't want you having a relapse."

Hattie sighed loudly as she left. It was always too damp, too windy, too something. Finishing breakfast, she fumbled in the sewing basket. *The sampler's bor-*

der would be nice in blue, she thought; *or maybe the cottage in the center*. Mama had suggested brown like their split-log home, but blue was Hattie's favorite color. Unlike her sister, who thought of little else, she wasn't concerned about finding a husband, and babies were too much trouble. However, she did want her own house someday, with a red barn and at least three horses . . .

Her daydream was interrupted by a knock on the front porch door. She recognized the voice of her school teacher and tried to look busy with embroidery as Miss Kate came in.

"Hi, Hattie. It's good to see you! How are you feeling?"

"Much better." She sat up straight against the lumpy feather pillows and pushed back her long mane, wishing she'd brushed it. Miss Kate was one of those folks who kept every tuck and black curl where it belonged. Hattie always felt a bit rumpled around her.

"That was quite an adventure you had. We've missed you at school."

"I've really missed school," she said honestly.

Miss Kate looked around. "What a delightful room. Whose embroidery?" She pointed to the colorful square on one wall.

"Rosalie's. So are the dress patterns." The bare cypress boards on her sister's side of the room were covered with them.

"And the horse?"

"That's Fonso. I found it in an old newspaper," Hattie said proudly. "He won the Kentucky Derby in 1880, the year I was born."

"I see," said Miss Kate, running her fingers along a U-shaped mahogany dressing table. Beautifully carved flowers framed the oval mirror, and a doilie embroidered with butterflies draped each side. A velvet-covered stool positioned close to the mirror was Rosalie's favorite perch.

"You must be proud of this. One doesn't usually see pieces like this around here."

"Mama's family brought it from Georgia. Most of their things were lost in the War."

"They homesteaded here?"

"No, ma'am. They sailed across the Gulf to Galveston. Then yellow fever broke out, and they all died there except Mama and Aunt Millie. They lived with friends until she met Papa. Gramma and Grandpa Marshall settled this place back when the neighbors were Indians. Wish I'd been around then."

"I understand your grandmother's quite a doctor. She says you'll be up soon. Meanwhile, I thought you might enjoy this . . ." She held out a large, red, leatherbound book.

Hattie took it eagerly, then sagged with disappointment.

"*Little Women?*"

Of the many books they could borrow from the school's back shelf, why this one? She'd been waiting a turn with *Treasure Island*, a new adventure story the boys had been excited about. And though she'd read them before, *Robinson Crusoe* or *Black Beauty* would have been welcome.

Miss Kate's dark eyes twinkled. "Give it a try, Hattie. There's a character I think you'll appreciate."

Hattie thanked her teacher politely as Miss Kate left, wondering what her remark was supposed to mean. *That's fine*, she thought. *Now I can choose between her ninny book and my sloppy sampler.* She stared through the blue gingham curtains to the beckoning yard. Enough was enough.

4

❖

Squirrels in the Tree

Hattie listened as the low rattle of Miss Kate's buggy faded up the road. Mama remained outside, and the house was silent. Hattie probed under the bed for her shoes—they weren't there. They must still be in the barn, where Papa had repaired and oiled them. She started to dig a pair of Sam's outgrown overalls from the trunk, then decided against it. No point in getting dressed. She would only be out for a few minutes.

Carefully she propped the window up with a stick and squeezed on through, dropping a short distance to the ground. The familiar feel of cold, sandy soil between her toes strengthened her resolve. She crouched down so she could peek under the house, which stood three feet off the ground. A brown mottled hen was scratching about in search of bugs. On the other side, near the creek, Hattie saw a small fire and a huge pot of boiling water. She knew Mama was washing clothes. *Good*, Hattie thought; no one would bother her for a while.

She walked carefully across the yard, now scattered with acorns, and approached the glistening, crimson tree. A low knot made a perfect foothold as she dug long fingers into the bark and hoisted herself up.

The lowest branch was easy to reach. She grabbed it with both hands and swung her feet around to hang upside-down possum-like in midair. With great effort she pulled herself up to straddle the branch, then rested before standing on trembly legs. Though she'd made this climb countless times, it had never been so hard; the illness had left her weaker than she realized. However, the next twenty feet was like scaling a ladder, and she soon settled in a familiar fork.

Hattie wearily propped her back against the tree and closed her eyes, wishing the red leaves would stop spinning. Her head pounded, and sweat dripped down her cheeks, darkening her nightdress. Maybe this wasn't such a good idea after all. . .

She was startled by a rustle of leaves and an acorn bouncing off her arm. A fat, gray squirrel scurried overhead. He paused to stare at her. Hattie held her breath, hoping he'd come closer. A sharp twittering from the tree trunk surprised her as another squirrel raced past her elbow to join its mate.

"You're a brave little rascal," she said as the noisy pair vacated the tree. "Don't worry, I can't stay long."

Through the leaves, she could see portions of the cotton field. Rosalie's yellow bonnet and Sam's black hat stood in contrast to the snowy blanket of cotton. *She must be wearing his ears out*, thought Hattie as her sister's hands waved vigorously. She grinned. "I'll bet Sam's ready for me to get well, too."

A faint crackling from the field behind the barn told her that Papa was pulling up the corn left to dry for meal. Closer were soft splashing sounds as Mama and Gramma rinsed hot lye soap from the laundry. A line of white shirts and sheets already fluttered in the morning breeze. Feeling better now, Hattie stretched and breathed deeply.

A shrill whistle pierced the crisp air as a wagon rumbled into view. Hattie strained to see who was on board, then recognized a black and tan streak—the McKinneys' coonhound, who was running on ahead despite Vince's whistle to stay with them. Vince was evidently driving his mother over to call.

"Mama won't like having her wash interrupted twice in one morning." Hattie scrambled to her feet. "And I'd better get inside."

She began climbing down, which was slower going than on the way up, when the dog's bay grew louder. Hattie looked between her bare feet in dismay. The eager hound had found her trail and was barking up the tree in triumph.

"Hush, girl! Go chase a rabbit." Trying to hurry, Hattie caught her sleeve on a branch. *Rip-p-p-p*...

"Oh no," she groaned, trying to free the muslin without doing further damage. "Hush up, Colleen!"

"What's the matter with you, Colleen? That's no coon—though what it is, I ain't sure."

Hattie jumped at the deep voice. She looked down at Vince's broad, freckled face and mischievous, brown eyes. She gathered the nightdress closer around her and tried not to look embarrassed, but her face felt as bright as the leaves.

"Would you please hush that hound?"

"What for? She's supposed to bay when she's treed a varmint."

"Well, this varmint's coming down, so move back. If you're looking for Sam, he's in the cotton field."

Vince didn't move. "I thought you were too sick to be shimmying up trees."

"I'm fine, but nobody believes it. Couldn't stand another day in that room." She stood on the lowest limb. "And I can't do this with you gawking!"

"Maw wanted to look in on you," he continued. "I could save her a trip inside."

"No! Mama's going to skin me!" Frustrated, she flung an acorn at his head. "Now go away!"

Vince ducked. A second acorn stung his ear.

"Oh, all right. Guess I could head 'em off for you." He ambled toward the house, turning to grin wickedly.

Hattie jumped to the ground as he rounded the corner. She could hear Vince buying her some time.

"Don't worry, Mrs. Alice, Colleen didn't give your

hens a second look. Would you have any biscuits left this morning?"

Squeezing through the window, Hattie heard Mrs. McKinney complain about boys' appetites. *She should know, after raising five of 'em*, thought Hattie, relieved that they'd stopped in the kitchen.

After dusting the grit from her cold, bare feet, she dove into bed. With the covers pulled to her chin, she felt safe for the moment. The sleeve would have to be fixed before Mama saw it. For once she was glad to have the sewing kit.

5

❖

Hard Freeze

Once Gramma had pronounced her well again, Hattie thought she would never get caught up with schoolwork and late harvest. There were pumpkins, pecans, dried corn, and late peas—food everywhere needing to be picked, shelled, or shucked. She hardly noticed that the squirrels had filled their pantry and disappeared or that the livestock had grown extra woolly—until she awoke one morning to a frozen world.

A rainstorm the night before had hardened to a crystal coating of ice on her window. She shivered as her bare feet hit the cold boards. Rosalie turned over, adding Hattie's share of the covers to her own cocoon. Hattie dressed quickly and stepped out into the breezeway, anxious to nestle by the fireplace, when *thud!*—she went down hard when her stockings slipped on the icy floor.

"What fell?"

"Anybody hurt?"

Heads appeared from the other doors that

opened onto the wide breezeway. Gramma's bedroom and Sam's were on either side of Hattie's. Their parents' room joined the large kitchen across the eight-foot breezeway. It was a simple construction, airy and practical—except in bad weather.

"Be careful. Rain blew in, and the whole floor is slick," said Mama. "Papa's going to salt it down after he breaks the ice on the water trough."

Sam hoisted Hattie upright as she rubbed her backside.

"We'll fix the floor later. Maybe we should fix Hattie first," he teased.

"Rosalie, put some shoes on before you come out here," called Gramma.

Hattie stepped gingerly to the kitchen, then scurried over to the crackling fire. She backed up as close to the flames as she could, arching her back as the friendly heat soaked into her bones. Her nose wrinkled, drinking in the smells of coffee and frying bacon. Surely this was the best part of winter.

Sam felt otherwise. Wiping moisture off the window, he stared at the clear, sapphire sky that had been created by the cold front.

"That norther' sure messed up our turkey hunt. The woods will be too quiet now."

"The Good Lord must get tired of trying to please folks," chuckled Gramma. "Some yearn for days just like this, while others want foul weather."

He smiled. "I'm not complaining, Gramma. I'm just anxious for some of your turkey and dressing."

"So am I," Hattie chimed in.

"Me too. By the way, Hattie, you need to crack some pecans before next week," reminded Mama.

"I don't know what good that will do. She eats as many as she shells." Rosalie slammed the door with a shiver.

"Maybe *you'd* like to do it," retorted Hattie, stuffing her mouth full of bacon.

"Sorry . . .I'm working on a new lace collar."

Hattie was disdainful. "And why might you need that, sister dear?"

"The Shelleys are having a party for Ida. She'll be sixteen next month."

"I suppose Lester Forbes will be there," said Hattie, batting her eyes.

Rosalie ignored her and went on, "By the way, Mama, I invited Lester to come over for Thanksgiving."

"You what?" exclaimed Hattie. "Why doesn't he stay home with his own folks?"

"They're visiting family over in Tyler. Someone had to tend the store." Rosalie turned an appealing face to Mama. "I should have asked first, but I ran into him in town and didn't think you'd mind."

"It'll be all right," she replied, giving Gramma a knowing look.

"Well, Sam, you'd better fetch *two* turkeys," said Hattie in disgust. "And I'll hide the pecan pie 'cause he can eat one of those by himself."

"Hush," said Rosalie, turning a faint pink. "And if you're rude to Lester, you'll be real sorry."

Hattie gathered the breakfast scraps onto one plate. "I'm already sorry," she muttered.

After sharing breakfast with the three cats nestled in the barn, Hattie set about milking the family's two longhorn cows. She huddled against Esther's warm, round belly and sprayed long, white streams into the tin pail. Sweet-smelling steam rose from the foamy milk as Esther munched her corn.

Hattie knew that the other cow, Vashti, would be another story. She'd kick if you just looked at her cross-eyed. Hattie placed her stool as far as possible from the bony hind legs. Vashti was known to make sudden moves whenever someone touched her.

When the cow refused to give any milk Hattie pled, "C'mon, old cow, my hands aren't that cold."

The white head shook in defiance.

Hattie stroked Vashti's side, warming her fingers in the thick winter coat. "Easy, girl. Just think about your breakfast."

A door slammed at the house. Hattie hoped no one would startle the fidgety cow with any more sudden noises like that. Just as the first squirt of milk hit the pail, Hattie heard a loud cry. Vashti jumped, knocking over both bucket and stool, but not before Hattie leaped for the door.

The sight that met her nearly made her choke. Gramma lay sprawled on the bottom of the icy porch steps. Hattie rushed over to her just as Mama appeared at the door.

"Good heavens! Gramma, hold still. . . . Hattie, find Papa."

Hattie stood frozen, transfixed by the wrinkled face twisted in pain. Gramma was moaning but hadn't opened her eyes. Mama gently felt her frail-looking limbs.

"Rosalie, get some blankets out here," she cried. "Hattie, move, girl!"

Feeling as if she'd been struck a physical blow, Hattie turned to race for the back pasture where the men were tending stock.

"Papa!" she screeched. "Papa! Sam! Come quick! . . . Gramma's hurt. Papa . . . !"

At the close of the second longest day of her life, Hattie huddled by the fireplace, quietly poking the embers. It had taken Sam hours to find the county's only doctor. Dusk had fallen before she heard heavy steps in the hall and was ordered to stay in the kitchen. Though they had tried to make Gramma comfortable, her moans echoed again and again in Hattie's head.

"Please, God, let her be all right," she prayed over and over. The alternative was unthinkable.

Rosalie started a fresh pot of coffee and put away the supper no one felt like eating. Hattie jumped to her feet as the door opened. Papa gave her a reassuring pat.

"Gramma's hip is broken, and she'll be down a while," he said. "But that's the worst of it."

"Can I talk to her?"

"She's asleep. You can take the doc some coffee though."

Rosalie filled an unchipped china cup, and Hattie tiptoed into Gramma's room. She listened to the quiet breathing and Mama questioning the doctor in low tones. She watched in awe as he packed shining instruments into a black leather case. Candlelight glowed through curly, brown hair that was growing thin on top.

"Dr. Siegen . . ." she whispered, offering him the hot cup.

"Hmm? Ah, thank you." The bushy eyebrows knit curiously as he studied her face. "Have I had the pleasure?"

"I'm Hattie," she said, suddenly feeling shy. "I go to school with Eric."

"Of course. He has mentioned a becoming young lady named Marshall."

Her face turned warm. "That must be my sister," she said shyly. "How long will Gramma have to stay in bed?"

"Many weeks, I'm afraid. Older people heal slowly. She will need a great deal of attention and cheering up so she doesn't get discouraged. Can you help her in this way?"

"Yes, sir," Hattie said, straightening a bit.

"Very good." He winked, and the long sideburns curled as he smiled. "Now I must go home and instruct my Eric on how to talk to girls."

Hattie grinned, liking this first doctor she had ever met. She appreciated his warm manner and funny accent, and especially the fact that he was looking after Gramma. It wasn't until he left that she noticed another, smaller figure in the room. Golden braids wound like a halo around a pale, delicate face she had never seen before.

Hattie held her breath, remembering stories about angels coming to aid God's people in special times of need. Surely if anyone deserved an angel, it was Gramma. But that was silly. Angels had wings and would never wear calico.

Mama noticed her staring. "Hattie, this is the doctor's niece. She's learning to be a nurse."

Deep violet eyes that absorbed and reflected the candlelight turned toward her. The girl offered a slim hand. "I'm Lorene Kohlmann."

"Oh," said Hattie with relief. "Don't you have to go to school to be a nurse?"

"My parents thought it wise to work with Uncle Josef a while before I enroll in nursing school," she said tiredly. "To get the whole picture."

"It's been a long day for everyone," said Mama. "Lorene, will you have some coffee before you go?"

"Can I sit with Gramma?" asked Hattie.

45

"I was hoping you would," replied Mama, leading Lorene to the kitchen.

Hattie settled into her grandmother's caneback rocker, close to the bed. The candle threw flickering shadows across Gramma's sweet, lined face, tense even in slumber. Hattie had never injured a bone. *It must hurt something awful*, she thought, *to be broken on the inside*. Despite the doctor's reassurance, a different fear than she had ever known gripped her.

All her life, Gramma had been there with a warm hug and an understanding word, putting up with Hattie's shenanigans when Mama's patience was long gone. Hot tears filled her eyes, making the candlelight seem dim. If anything worse happened to Gramma, she didn't know what she'd do.

6

❖

A Time of Thanks

The following days blurred together in Hattie's mind. Despite the doctor's optimism, Gramma was in considerable pain. And Hattie shared the hurt, hoping somehow to ease Gramma's burden by her constant presence. Since Mama welcomed the help, Hattie was relieved of other chores, and a cot for Hattie was placed near Gramma's bed. A wood stove kept the room cozy, and a large window gave ample light for reading.

Gramma had been trying to get Hattie to read the Bible all the way through, and this seemed to be a good time to start—aloud, so they could enjoy the Bible passages together. They had survived the plagues of Exodus and were wandering with the Israelites one gray afternoon when Hattie noticed that Gramma's eyes were closed. Hattie stopped to listen, for she had learned to tell the change in Gramma's breathing when she was asleep.

"You want me to stop now?" she asked.

"No, honey. Listening to you helps me forget these

47

old bones." The weary, blue eyes opened. "But you must be tired of sitting. Go visit your critters awhile."

"That's okay. I can read another chapter."

"What about your book?" It turned out that Gramma enjoyed *Little Women*, which Miss Kate had insisted that Hattie finish.

Hattie shrugged.

"Don't you like it?" asked Gramma.

"Well, city girls have some odd ways." Hattie thought a minute. "Meg's too much like Rosalie—always bossy and nit-picking."

The echo of a dimple creased Gramma's parchment-like cheek.

"Jo makes more sense than any of them. She's just herself."

"Like someone else I know."

"Ma'am?"

"Never mind. Who does little Amy remind you of?"

"Ida Shelley. She's such a prisspot."

"What about the other one?"

Hattie paused. It pained her to read about Beth, the quiet sister who had suffered scarlet fever and had not fully recovered. She worried about Beth's future, because the story seemed to hint of sadder things to come. Beth was perfectly sweet, and everyone loved her—the kind of person Hattie wanted to be but had given up trying. Hattie couldn't think of anyone to compare her with, except perhaps Gramma, and she wasn't comfortable with that.

"I don't know, Gramma. She's too good."

"Sounds like she won't be with them much longer."

"She might get well yet."

"Everyone has to go sometime, Hattie."

"But not when they're young or when people need them. That wouldn't make sense."

"The Good Lord isn't obliged to explain Himself," Gramma said. "Your Grandpa went when he was still a young man and we needed him."

Hattie rocked in silence, thinking about the grandfather she only knew from the tintype of a tall, thin man in his gray, Confederate uniform.

"How did you feel about that?" she asked.

Grandma thought a moment. "Mad as a hornet. That hurt was like a knife turning inside when I thought about him, which was most of the time. This broken hip can't come close." She paused, and her voice sounded faraway.

"There was this place to look after, your Aunt Julia was small, and no one had money after the war. It was hardest on your papa, him being thirteen. But I'm glad Andrew was the oldest. He handled the situation better than most would have."

"How long did you stay mad?"

"Oh . . . months, I guess. I wouldn't talk to God, not even to say grace at the table. The children thought I'd gone peculiar." Gramma sighed as she gazed out the window. "But then we had a fair crop, and one day when we finished getting the corn in, it hit me—He was still looking out for us. The children were healthy, we had food for the winter, and we couldn't ask for better neighbors. It was like those Israelites wandering in the desert for years. They faced a heap of changes and had to depend on the Good Lord for every meal, but He was always there looking out for them. Why, I just sat down by the corncrib and cried and thanked Him for loving us."

Her eyes glistened as she looked at Hattie. "The knife was gone after that. I still missed your Grandpa, but I knew he was all right and that we would be too."

Hattie was quiet a while. "Gramma, I didn't mean that folks have to be young for us to need them. We need you something awful."

Gramma's thin, mottled hand patted the smooth, brown one. "I know what you meant."

"Do you look forward to seeing him again?"

"Who? Your grandpa?"

Hattie nodded, almost afraid of the answer.

"Why, sure I do. Spending forever with those we love is one of the best things about heaven. But I'm in no hurry—I have to see you grown-up and married first."

Hattie rolled her eyes. "Well, that may take a while!"

They both laughed. It felt so good to laugh with Gramma again.

❖

50

Sam and Vince spent the next morning in the woods, returning with four acorn-fat turkeys. Rosalie dusted and scrubbed every corner of the family room, and furniture was moved so Gramma's bed would fit in the corner. She was feeling "a mite better" and couldn't bear the thought of Thanksgiving dinner being fixed without her. Though not allowed to sit up, she managed to chop celery in a shallow pan. Hattie sat beside her shelling pecans and eating only a handful. Mama, up to her elbows in dressing, looked cross.

"Rosalie, stop fussing over those pictures. Lester will be more concerned about what's on his plate than what's hanging on the wall. Fetch and peel the apples."

Hattie cackled as Rosalie stomped out.

"Now, Hattie, you get a pound of butter from the cooler and the can of brown sugar."

She obeyed promptly.

"All right, now wash your hands. I only have two, so you can put the pecan pie together."

"Do what?"

"You're old enough to make a pie."

"But, Mama . . ."

"Just do as I tell you. Set the butter on the stove to soften," she ordered. "Now take about half that ball of dough and sprinkle some flour there." Mama was giving directions with her right elbow.

"Put the dough in the middle and flour the rolling pin . . . Good . . . Now work out from the cen-

51

ter . . . You're doing it . . . Now turn and roll the other way . . . Hattie, you've seen this done a hundred times," she said in exasperation.

"But, Mama, I wasn't *watching*."

"Well, remember, it has to end up round."

Hattie clumsily pushed the wooden rolling pin this way and that. The supple dough would lie quietly a moment, then slowly pull itself together. Finally it grew larger than the pie plate. Rosalie returned and watched in shocked silence.

"Now what?" asked Hattie.

"Put it in the plate."

"How do I pick it up?"

"Carefully."

Hattie pried one side up with her fingers and lifted ever so slowly. The thin dough pulled free of the surface as her hand slipped under the fragile middle. But the other edge decided to stick, and a large crack quickly appeared.

"Mama!"

"It's all right," she soothed. "Just put it on the plate. You can fix that."

"How?" Hattie wailed.

"Wet your fingers, and mash the dough together," answered Mama. "The bottom doesn't show anyway."

Hattie's mouth was set tight as she repaired the crack and sighed with relief. "What about the edges?"

Mama cleaned her hands and gave a three-fingered pinch to the dough humped on the plate's edge. "Do this all the way around, then trim off what's hanging over."

Hattie squeezed the soft dough between her thumb and first two fingers. Decorative peaks magically appeared as she circled the plate. This part was easier than it looked, she thought. She trimmed the sides and stood back proudly.

"Look, Gramma."

"That's mighty fine." Gramma wasn't looking at the pie crust but at Mama, whose eyes held the same mischievous gleam. Mama didn't look mischievous very often. Hattie wondered what it meant.

"It's beautiful," Mama said, giving Hattie's flour-smudged cheek a kiss. "Now let's get the filling in."

Hattie was doubtful that she could manage that, but she followed Mama's directions for the right amounts of butter, syrup, eggs, flour, and pecans. At last the pie was complete. She hovered protectively near the oven as it baked, watching Rosalie expertly turn out two more crusts. These were filled with apples, sugar, and cinnamon.

"Lester Forbes will have to eat apple," said Hattie.

"What?"

"I said Lester can't have my pie. It's just enough for us."

"He can have anything he wants," Rosalie snapped.

"Hattie, it's not polite to tell company what they can and can't eat," said Mama.

"I don't care." Hattie set her jaw. "It's mine, and he can't have it."

Mama sighed as Gramma spoke up. "Rosalie, one pecan pie probably isn't enough anyway. You have time to make another."

By dinnertime the next day, Rosalie had cooked that and much more. Even Sam noticed how industrious she had become and suspected it was to impress "poor ole Lester." Hattie was sure of that and lost no opportunity to badger her sister.

"You know, this table's too crowded with food to fit an extra plate on it. Can't we just put him on the porch?"

"No, but you can go there yourself," suggested Rosalie.

"It's Thanksgiving," said Mama. "We will all sit together."

As Hattie shuffled plates around, she heard hoofbeats. Rosalie glanced at her image in a pane of glass, pinning up a stray curl and straightening her apron. Hattie hoped she'd never be caught making such a fuss over some boy—over *any* boy. She watched as Rosalie opened the door with a flourish and displayed her sweetest smile.

"Hello, Lester, we're so glad you could join us today."

Hattie rolled her eyes at Gramma while the others greeted their guest. He appeared to have spent as much time primping as Rosalie had. The straight, coal-black hair was slicked back so tight Hattie thought it would break. The black string tie hung a bit crooked against the glaring white shirt his mother must have starched before she left, and the fine plaid coat looked odd in the homey surroundings.

Built more like a logger than a storekeeper, Lester looked normal enough waiting on customers in his shirt-sleeves. Even at church when everyone else was dressed up, his special-order city clothes were all right. But not here.

It suddenly hit Hattie what her sister saw in this awkward young man. Miss Everything-has-to-be-perfect Fussbudget Marshall wanted to be Mrs. Forbes General Mercantile! She could imagine Rosalie strutting about in every new dress that came in, deciding which ones to keep for herself. Hattie wanted to shout, to warn Lester of the trap he was stepping into. He really wasn't a bad sort. Certainly he didn't deserve Rosalie!

The friendly chatter continued as Lester paid his respects to Gramma and everyone sat down to dinner. It was indeed a table over which to be thankful. The largest of Sam's turkeys had baked to a crisp golden-bronze, its clear juices trickling over the bed of cornbread dressing. Beside it sat the spouted blue-and-white bowl filled with pungent giblet gravy, Hattie's favorite. Glossy orange sweet potatoes swam in thick cane syrup next to Mama's best china bowls filled with butter beans, field peas, and mustard greens. A red checkered cloth kept the buttermilk rolls warm, and four pies sat temptingly on the sideboard. Hattie planned to serve *her* pecan herself.

Her stomach growled as Papa gave thanks for the bountiful meal and Gramma's improving health. She peeked to see if anyone else had heard it. Well, Rosalie and Lester surely hadn't. With heads bowed and eyes glued to each other, he had reached over to squeeze her hand. Hattie cleared her throat as they both jumped and Papa said, "Amen."

The Marshall clan plus one dug in. It was a feast to remember.

That evening the house was filled with neighbors checking on Gramma, Dr. Siegen's family among them. His wife was taller than he and was stooped slightly, as if to make up for it. Her faded golden hair was braided in the same manner as her niece's. Lorene said little, giving the same impression of warmth and quiet confidence that Hattie had noticed before.

Eric, blond like his mother, fidgeted by the fireplace. As he talked with Sam, his eyes followed Rosalie and Lester washing the dishes. Hattie shook her head. Though smart and pleasant enough, he was barely fourteen and was far beneath her sister's notice.

"Young man, I've looked after myself for near sixty years without calling a doctor," Gramma was protesting.

"We all need help sometimes, dear lady," the

doctor said kindly. "Now, let Lorene and me look at your feet."

"My feet! Why would anybody want to see these poor, old, bony feet? What do they teach in those schools anyhow?"

Hattie sipped her hot cider and watched in amusement until she turned to Sam. He was watching, too, with the same faraway look as when he saw a deer in the forest or geese flying overhead. Puzzled, she followed his gaze back to the doctor checking... no, to his nurse checking Gramma. Hattie had to admit that Lorene looked pretty in the firelight. With that thought, something pulled tight in her stomach. No longer amused, she noisily gathered the dessert plates.

"Here you go," she said, dropping them in the soapy water.

"What ... More?" Rosalie pushed a damp wisp of hair back with her arm. "I need some air," she said, taking off her apron. "You can finish those."

Before Hattie had time to sputter, Rosalie and Lester vanished and made a bee-line to the porch. Hattie almost protested to Mama, but Mama was talking with Mrs. Siegen and wouldn't like being interrupted.

Hattie debated a moment. She concluded that being a martyr would look more grown-up than complaining. With her shoulders slumped, she plunged her hands into the pan. Imagine—making her wash dishes on a holiday . . .

7

❖

Christmas Belles

December brought more company, food, and dishes, some of which Hattie could not avoid dealing with. The doctor stopped by often, always wearing his broad smile and fishing a peppermint from his bag. Sam would manage to finish whatever chore he was doing and come in for coffee. Hattie thought she knew why, but then once he was in the house he hardly spoke to Lorene beyond saying hello.

Since Ida Shelley's birthday fell near Christmas, her mother always made it a holiday event. Though the entire Marshall clan was invited, only Rosalie was expected to attend this year. She finished her new outfit early one morning and spent the rest of the day fussing with her hair.

"When's Lester coming?" asked Hattie.

"Around 4, so we can be there before dark. Help me with this, will you?" She backed up so Hattie could cinch up her corset.

Hattie pulled the slack out of the strings as Rosalie sucked in her breath. Rosalie held it in while

Hattie looped the strings around metal hooks and tied a bow.

"Make a double knot," said Rosalie. "I'd hate to bend over and pop loose."

"How can you bend with those bone things sticking in your middle?"

"They're called stays. A corset wouldn't support much if they weren't sewn in there." Rosalie tried to take another deep breath and seemed satisfied when she couldn't. Studying her figure in the oval mirror, she put the bustled petticoat on next.

Hattie shook her head and cackled, "First you cinch up beyond breathing, and then you tie a wire contraption on your rump. You look like a horse packed for a trip."

Rosalie looked scornful as she pulled on her outer petticoat and soft, lacy camisole. "The nicest dress in the world would look tacky without the proper undergarments," she quipped, slipping a bundle of emerald-green velvet over her head. It was her first and only velvet dress; the fabric was picked exclusively to match her eyes.

"Button me up," she ordered, holding the new crocheted collar in place. She was obviously pleased with her reflection in the mirror. "So what do you think?"

It was a pretty picture, but Hattie would have choked before saying so. "How do you expect to eat, much less dance, in that get-up?"

"Carefully," said Rosalie. "Just wait, little girl, your turn's coming."

Hattie harrumphed. "When pigs fly."

"You're just out of sorts because you're not going."

"That's silly. Why would I want to?"

"Because some of your friends will be there, and there'll be music and all kinds of delicious food." Rosalie carefully tied a green hair bow. "Besides, it's time you learned to dance."

"Not me, thank you."

"Hattie's too young to be staying up all night," put in Mama as she opened the door.

"If she really wants to go, I'll bring her home before too late," came a voice from the porch.

"I didn't know you were going," said Hattie. Her mouth dropped open as Sam came in. Though he wore the same crisp white shirt and dark blue pants as on Sunday, there was a difference. The dark brown hair was combed to perfection, the tie was even instead of lopsided, and something glowed deep in his eyes.

She wrinkled her nose as a spicy fragrance filled the room.

"Hoo-eee, what's that?"

Sam grinned. "Must be a polecat under the house. Do you want to ride with me to Shelleys'?"

Hattie struggled inside. Though they couldn't have paid her to ride with Lester and Rosalie, Sam's going changed things. It wasn't that she didn't like parties—she enjoyed music and sweets. Until recently she had loved the chance to eat and visit with friends. But now all those friends cared about was clothes and hair and who liked whom.

The girls would giggle and watch the boys, who ate too much and elbowed one another until some brave soul asked a girl to dance. Then the pair would look awkward and embarrassed while everyone stared—until one by one the others found their nerve. Soon only a few would be left to watch.

Hattie knew she would be one of those. Even if a boy did ask, she hadn't learned to dance and wasn't about to make a fool of herself trying.

"I guess not," she said finally.

"Are you sure?" said Mama. "I don't mind you going if Sam's there."

Hattie slowly shook her head and retreated to the kitchen.

Soon Lester's buggy was heard outside, and he and Rosalie were off. The house seemed unusually quiet as the rest of them ate supper, the empty places at the table matching the feeling in Hattie's chest. Her bowl of stew had no taste at all.

"Aren't you hungry?" asked Mama.

She shrugged and tried to force down a potato. It wouldn't go. "I guess not," she said.

Mama felt her cheek and looked at her intently. Sometimes it felt like Mama could look straight through to her bones.

"No fever," she said. "Want to lie down awhile?"

"Yes'm." Hattie walked listlessly to the door.

"I'm working on some Christmas items after supper. Think you'll feel like helping?"

"I'll try," she said weakly.

Crossing the cold breezeway to her room, she flopped across the bed. Rosalie's powder and hairpins were still strewn on the dresser. Seeing them made the lonely ache even worse. Why did they all have to grow up and change?

She dug out Miss Kate's book, *Black Beauty*. That poor horse had more troubles than any animal she knew, but thinking about other folks' problems sometimes helped you forget your own.

The party-goers returned the next morning, bleary-eyed but cheerful. Hattie was waiting for them in the porch rocker.

"Well, how was it?" she asked.

"Wonderful!" Rosalie exclaimed. "I've never danced so much in my whole life." She waited as Lester tied the team and helped her climb down. "Are the folks up?"

"I should say so," drawled Hattie. "The day's half gone."

Lester pulled out his gold pocket watch, looking puzzled. "It's only 8:30."

"Pay her no mind," Rosalie cooed, taking his arm.

Hattie ambled to the barn, where Sam was feeding Chica.

"Mama saved you some breakfast," she said.

"I wouldn't know where to put it." He yawned. "Mrs. Shelley could've fed an army."

"Did you have a good time?"

"Sure did," he said, brushing Chica's thick winter coat. "You should've come."

"Maybe next time. Were the Siegens there?"

"Yep. Eric asked about you."

Hattie grimaced. "Did you dance with anybody?"

Sam hung up the brush, stretched, and yawned again. "Seems like."

Hattie folded her arms and scowled. "Well, who?"

An overnight growth of whiskers made Sam's dimples even deeper as he grinned. "Watch out, Hattie—you're sounding like Rosalie."

"Oh, never mind." Hattie stomped to the house, where her sister would be telling all. She'd find out what she wanted to know there. Instead she was met by smiles and hugs.

"What's going on?"

"It's about time you came in to hear the news," said Rosalie. She took Lester's arm and looked up adoringly. "We're going to be married."

Hattie stared at their tired, beaming faces. She couldn't think of anything to say or do for a moment. She felt like she was made out of wood.

"Well, aren't you going to congratulate them?" asked Mama.

Hattie drew herself up to full height, which was

a good three inches taller than Rosalie, and stuck out a wooden hand.

"Congratulations, big sister," she said solemnly.

Rosalie laughed and took the hand. Nothing could spoil her mood today.

Hattie turned somber eyes to Lester. "Congratulations, you poor soul. I've lived with her twelve years and four months, and it's no picnic."

"Hattie!" Mama protested.

Lester's hamlike hand swallowed Hattie's slim, brown one as he laughed. "Maybe you can advise me."

She nodded thoughtfully and went back to the porch, away from the happy chatter of newly hatched plans. There she sank in a rocker and watched Sam saunter in from the barn.

"They're getting hitched," she said.

"So they broke the news." He paused to study her glum face. "What's wrong?"

"Lester's not a bad sort. But he has no idea . . ." Hattie leaned forward to whisper, "She's just after the store."

Sam chuckled. "If that were so, she probably wouldn't be the first."

He propped against the porch post and rubbed his bristles. "But seriously, I wouldn't go around saying that. Rosalie's been raised better, and Mama wouldn't appreciate the rumor."

Hattie shook her head. Sometimes Sam just didn't seem to understand.

Sam went on, "Look at it this way—Lester would be a good husband if he didn't have a dime. He's honest and hard-working and appreciates the way she is. You've got to admit, Rosalie's a fine cook, and kind of pretty when she's not being a pain. Anyhow, has it occurred to you they might really love each other?"

Hattie grunted. "She's such a fussbudget."

"So's his mama. He's used to it." He grinned and pulled her away from the rocker. "Speaking of the mercantile, want to go Christmas shopping?"

"Really? I don't have any money."

"I have a few dollars tucked away. Get dressed while I shave and slosh down some coffee."

Two hours later they entered an unusually busy Forbes General Mercantile. Hattie paused to drink in the aroma of apple and cinnamon, cloves and leather, mingled with other delightful scents she couldn't name. She noticed a cluster of older girls giggling at the millinery counter; an innocent sprig of mistletoe hung overhead. Avoiding that spot, she stopped to examine a collection of gadgets and cooking utensils.

"Sam, look here . . ." She pointed to a funny-looking contraption. "It's a corn sheller. Think Papa would like that?"

He studied the device. "It would save wear on the hands."

Hattie agreed. She hated shelling the bushels of hard corn left to dry for meal and animal feed.

"Maybe Papa would like it," he said. "Now, can you find a warm shawl for Gramma?"

Hattie sorted through a stack of colorful woolen shawls. Choosing two, she found Sam hovering over the jewelry counter.

"What do you think?" she interrupted, holding up the shawls. "Peach or blue?"

"Whatever," he said absently, watching Mrs. Forbes pull another box from beneath the counter.

Hattie peeked over his shoulder at three necklaces in a green velvet case—two cameos and a porcelain rose.

"Who's that for?" she asked.

"Uh . . . I don't know. Think Mama would like one?"

"The cameo looks more like Rosalie. You know Mama. She likes anything we give her."

"That's true," he said, holding the tiny, pink rose by its delicate gold chain. It looked lost in his large, callused hand. "Maybe Mama would rather get a new bonnet."

"I guess," said Hattie. "She's sure set on me wearing one."

"Okay, you're the expert then."

Hattie shrugged and studied the rack of bonnets. Though she'd rather shop for something besides clothes, buying presents was a rare treat. Even if Sam was paying for them, hers was the work and worry of decision-making. By the time she carefully wrapped the gifts in brown paper and colorful yarn, the gifts would be just as much from her as from him.

Settling on a lavender and lace bonnet that would match Mama's Sunday dress, she called to Sam, "How's this one?"

He looked back from the counter and nodded, then returned to studying the jewelry. Why was he so concerned with choosing a gift for Rosalie? She shrugged it off and wandered to the end of the store reserved for tack and leather goods. The sweet, oily smell filled her head as she fingered silver conchos on a new saddle. What could Papa use the most?

Sam finally joined her. "All right, squirt, what are you spending my life savings on now?"

"Don't you think Papa needs a fancy Spanish saddle for rounding up hogs?" she asked.

"Sure, and a bridle to match." He laughed, lifting a silver-embossed headpiece from the wall. "Imagine a horse packing this on his head. Why, it must weigh twenty pounds. Maybe Papa would settle for the corn sheller."

Hattie agreed.

A few minutes later, after buying the gifts and after much deliberation at the candy counter, they left with a bag of chocolate bonbons and their hearts full of Christmas spirit.

Hattie's holiday joy lasted all through the week as she decorated the house with holly and pine boughs and helped Sam cut down a tree. She spent a whole afternoon dressing it with carefully strung popcorn, small red apples, and sweet gum balls dipped in colored candle wax. The balls were her idea—and the only decoration that would last until next year.

If keeping the gifts a secret was hard, waiting to open her own was torture. They mysteriously appeared one morning, including a large, lumpy one that she couldn't figure out. Her curiosity threatened to drive her crazy.

Finally Christmas Eve arrived with a hard freeze and treacherous roads that prevented the usual visits and caroling. Since Gramma couldn't ride to church, it was decided they would all stay home. Hattie was disappointed, and Rosalie fretted over not seeing Lester, but Sam was the most restless.

"Son, you're going to wear a rut in the floor," Mama said. "Sit down and have some pecan cake. It's still warm."

He sighed and perched on a stool, one foot tapping the floor. Then his face brightened.

"Gramma, how's your medicine holding out?"

She looked surprised. "That stuff the doc gave me? I still have some. 'Course it's not as good as my tonic, but I can't make more of that till spring. You children couldn't find the plants now."

"That's true," he agreed. "And with the roads frozen, Doc may not get here for a while. I could pick it up for you though."

"Well, that's mighty thoughtful, Sam, but I don't need it today."

Gramma tried to sit up in protest as Sam grabbed his coat. Seeming to have a new understanding of the situation, she leaned back with a smile. "Then again . . . Wish the doc and his bunch a merry Christmas for me," she said.

"Yes, ma'am." He winked at her and rushed through the door with a cold blast of air.

"Wait a minute!" yelled Hattie. "You can't leave now. It's almost time to open presents."

"Be careful," called Mama, shaking her head.

Hattie just didn't understand people sometimes. But she knew there was nothing she could do about the situation.

As evening approached, it was Hattie's turn to pace from window to frosted window. "What's taking him so long?"

"I suspect he had more than one errand," chuckled Papa from his chair by the fire. "Want to try beating me at checkers?"

As a light dawned in Hattie's head, her frown grew deeper. "You mean he's off courting while we wait to have our Christmas?"

"Christmas isn't just presents, Hattie," Mama chided softly.

"I know . . . I know . . . It's Jesus' birthday."

"And a special time to spend with people we care about," said Mama, looking out the dark window as her voice trailed off. "When they don't live under the

69

same roof, that can mean getting out in bad weather."

Hattie grunted and set up the checkerboard. But her mind wasn't on the game. When she had lost half her checkers to Papa's three kings, they heard heavy footsteps on the porch. Two bundled forms burst through the door.

"Look what I found wandering up the road," laughed Sam.

"Lester!" squealed Rosalie.

"Couldn't keep me away," he said, giving her a quick kiss right in front of everybody.

Hattie was shocked! But figuring it was time to get on to more important things, she tugged on Sam's coat. "*Now* can we open our presents?"

"All right, girl. Do the honors," said Papa, settling in his chair by the fire.

Hattie didn't wait to be told twice and scurried over to the tree. She gave each person a package, watching with pleasure as Gramma admired the blue shawl and Mama tied on her new bonnet. Sam had suggested wrapping an ear of corn with Papa's sheller so he could try it out immediately. He did just that, and stray kernels flew across the room.

"That will go to the barn," laughed Mama. "What did you get, Hattie?"

Hattie proudly pulled on the bright red stockings Gramma had knitted and the soft, black, leather boots from Sam. She was saving the biggest package for last, the lumpy one from Mama and Rosalie.

"Oooh, this is beautiful!" squealed Rosalie from the corner.

Hattie thought she'd opened the cameo, but then something flashed on her finger.

"An engagement ring! Mama, look . . ." Rosalie pranced around the room as they all admired her treasure. Lester beamed, trying to look modest. Hattie had to admit that the delicate gold band topped with a glowing diamond was very pretty. But if you had to get married to have one, she'd do without.

Sam nudged her and pointed to the large, lumpy package. "What's in there?"

She carefully untied the ribbon, trying to guess. It was too light for books, and a game would be in a box. Maybe it was a new coat to match her boots . . .

"Hurry up," urged Rosalie.

"Nope," said Hattie. "I won't be thirteen till July, and I may not get another present before then. This gift is special, and I want to make the experience last."

By now everyone had stopped to watch. Inside the brown wrapping was a layer of pink tissue. It crackled softly as Hattie lifted the top layer. Beneath it lay a bundle of white taffeta ruffles. Her face fell as she lifted it from the wrapping.

"You'll look like a grown-up lady now," said Rosalie. "It's a real petticoat, bustle and all. Stand up so we can see if the length is right."

Hattie's cheeks grew hot as she tried to stuff the

embarrassing item back into the wrapping, wishing she could make it disappear. Instead she noticed something else underneath the petticoat. Suspiciously, she held it up by two fingers.

"*A corset*? Oh!" She dropped it like a hot coal. "How could you!" she cried, picking up the petticoat and corset and tearing across the room.

Rosalie's mouth dropped open as Mama looked at Gramma in dismay. Papa got up to poke the fire, and Sam thoughtfully watched Hattie slam the door.

She stood in the breezeway as an icy blast whipped on through, cooling her hot cheeks. It was bad enough to be growing every which way and needing more harness, but did they have to make out like it was some great honor? Besides, her old muslin underwear was fine. She wouldn't wear that stuff if they tied it on her!

Hattie was starting to shiver when her eyes grew bright with inspiration. She ran to the dark barn, stumbling over a cat on the way. There she found an empty burlap sack. Quickly she stuffed in the petticoat and corset, wrapping and all, and tied it with a string from a hay bale.

This she tied to a low beam with a cluster of other sacks. Papa kept his seed here, where it would be dry and safe from varmints. The bags wouldn't be disturbed before spring, giving her time to properly dispose of the offending garments. Maybe she'd bury them when the ground thawed. With her mouth set with grim satisfaction, she ran back to the house and was in bed when Mama came in.

"Are you warm enough?" she asked.

"Yes'm."

"We saved you some cake."

"I'll eat it tomorrow."

Mama stood quietly. Hattie felt a knot growing in her throat, and she wished Mama would go away.

"Hattie, we didn't mean to embarrass you. I thought about putting that present aside when Lester came, so you could open it later. I just wasn't quick enough."

"It's not just that," Hattie mumbled.

Mama sat on the bed. "What then?"

Hattie took a deep breath. Was it worth trying to make her understand? "Well, Christmas only comes once a year, and I'd imagined other things in that package and . . . and . . ." She choked back a loud sob. ". . . and I hate being a girl!"

"I know, honey," said Mama, stroking her hair. "Growing up takes a lot of getting used to. But God made you a girl, Hattie Belle, and He doesn't make mistakes. Try to accept that."

"Girls have to do such dumb stuff," she protested. "Wear this, do that, don't burp . . . Mama, you keep trying to make me like Rosalie, and I can't be! I just can't be!"

Mama looked startled. "I haven't tried . . . Well, maybe sometimes I have." She sighed. Holding Hattie's hand, she looked her straight in the eye.

"If that's how it seems, then I'm sorry. Rosalie takes to domestic life like a duck to water. You're more like a wild filly I have to keep roping in. But I love you every bit as much, Hattie."

Hattie's eyes burned, and she couldn't look at Mama.

"Let's try not making it so hard on each other, all right, Hattie?"

Hattie wasn't sure what Mama had in mind, but it didn't matter right then. She just wanted a hug.

8

❖

Terror in the Swamp

Winter had come and gone, and it was early March now. The first breath of spring had already begun whispering to the piney woods. Though the sandy, red earth was still hard and cold, Hattie could almost feel it stirring, ready to rise up and burst through the swollen buds on all the trees around her. She felt the same way herself on mornings like this one.

She shifted her weight in Papa's creaky saddle and ducked as his stout, brown gelding took her under a low limb. Unmindful of her height, Itchy doggedly followed Chica's red rump along the faint path.

"Any sign of Colleen?" Vince called from behind.

"Nope," said Sam.

Vince whistled. They stopped and listened to the silence.

"Sure wish I'd kept her on a leash, in case she does hit that panther's trail."

"It could be on the far side of the county by now," said Sam.

"Do you think it's the same one that . . . as last year?" Hattie hated to remind Sam or even think about the day he had brought poor Dolly home cut to ribbons. The old blue tick hound had been part of their family as long as Hattie could remember, but Dolly was no match for the panther she'd disturbed over a fresh kill.

"Possibly," he said. "It has the same taste for pork."

"Yep, Paw's mighty upset about those sows." Vince whistled again.

"Did they have their babies yet?" Hattie asked.

Vince shook his head.

"Hey, what are those?" Hattie, hoping to prove herself a tracker, pointed to a sandbar below them. Sam slid his mare down the steep bank for a closer look.

"Bobcat," he called. Hattie was disappointed. He rode back up, giving her hat a tug.

"Keep looking, eagle eyes. You might be the one to find that cat yet."

The trail dropped gradually to the edge of a large swampy area, where the dark water sat still and cold.

"It's so quiet here," whispered Hattie.

"Everyone's still asleep," said Vince.

"Another month and it'll be lively enough," Sam commented, riding close to the water's edge.

"Shame we'll miss it," said Vince.

"What?" asked Hattie, thinking she'd missed something.

Sam scowled at his friend, who just pointed on ahead.

"See the gator mound by those cypress trees?" asked Vince.

Hattie studied the miniature mountain of mud and grass where a female alligator would lay her eggs in the summer. "I see it."

"I was here once when a coon tried robbing that nest while the mama was away. I couldn't see her, but she was out in the water, watching and listening. They're pretty smart, you know. Well, anyway, the little bandit busted that first egg and hadn't finished breakfast before a racket like you never heard broke loose. Mama Gator boiled water getting to shore and came out roaring with fire in her eyes."

"What happened to the coon?" Hattie asked.

"He was up a tree before you could blink," laughed Vince.

"It's hard to imagine," she said. "The gators I've seen were so still they looked like logs. Then they'd just grunt and swim away."

"That's the best kind," said Sam.

Hattie searched the mud for more cat prints, hoping she might find the long marks of an alligator's tail as well. She saw neither. Circling the swamp, they found other tracks left by deer, possum, raccoon, and fox. Just as they turned back toward the creek, a long, clear note, almost like a horn blowing, floated through the swamp—Colleen's howl.

"I hope she hasn't found that varmint by herself," said Vince. He spun his mare around on the narrow path and kicked her into a gallop. But the woods were too thick for such a hasty ride. He dodged a limb, only to be grabbed by a fat vine and yanked from the saddle. He landed with a thud, muttering things Hattie decided to ignore.

Sam plunged on. Nimble Chica darted through trees and palmetto as her rider leaned low against her neck. The soft splats of her hooves had faded away by the time Vince untangled himself and Hattie caught his horse. She laughed at his flustered, red face.

"It's not funny!" He swung into the saddle, his muddy pants making a funny *squish* sound. "I shouldn't have turned that hound loose."

Hattie sobered. "Maybe she's just after a coon."

The baying had grown fainter, so they rode on as fast as the woods allowed. Hattie dodged the blur of vines and branches that reached for her. One snagged her coat, and she was forced to stop or risk tearing the coat badly. Vince pushed on ahead.

"Wait!" she called. It was wasted breath. By the time she got untangled, he was gone. "He's probably not worth squat as a brother either," she grumbled, more annoyed than afraid. Sam would never leave her alone, dog or no dog.

Following the hoofprints in the wet ground, she

noticed a change in Colleen's call. It was growing louder and from the direction from which they had just come. Could the varmint be circling back toward the swamp?

Hattie was torn between trying to follow Vince or turning back. Her skin tingled with excitement at the thought of catching Colleen first. But there was also the possibility of getting lost and never hearing the end of it. Well, if she did lose her way, it would be Vince's fault.

She turned and carefully retraced their path, noting its twists and turns and any unusual trees. Sam had taught her much about the woods, but she was never allowed to go exploring alone. It would be different if she had her own horse instead of having to wait for those rare days when Papa didn't need Itchy.

"Aaroooo!"

Hattie jumped. It sounded like Colleen was right on top of her. Wide-eyed, she pulled the gelding up and looked around, straining to hear more. The swamp was hushed, as if waiting . . .

"Aarr-roo-o!"

Tree limbs crackled, and a tall clump of palmetto leaned toward her as a black shape leaped through the fan-shaped leaves. Startled by Hattie's presence, the creature twisted in midair and slid to a stop. The panther!

It hissed, crouching only a few feet away. Hattie could see muscles ripple like coiled springs under the sleek hide. For an instant she gasped at the eyes that seemed to shoot yellow fire. The gleaming fangs opened, and Hattie heard a piercing, human-like scream. It tore at her insides, and she screamed too.

The terrified gelding squealed and bolted, and Hattie urged him on, not caring which way he ran. The panther screamed behind them, and she expected the horse to fall at any moment, pulled down by the great cat tearing at his flanks.

They plunged on blindly, leaping over rotting logs and pools of black water, hurrying ever deeper into the swamp. She tried to look back once, only to have moss slap her head and snatch away her hat.

Finally, after a long while, Hattie pulled Itchy to a stop. Foam dripped from the bit, and his sides heaved, but he couldn't stand still. Wild-eyed and trembling, he kept prancing about.

"Easy, boy," she whispered to herself as much as to the horse. "I think we're okay now."

Hattie tried to get her bearings. It was no use; nothing looked familiar. Even the sun was no help, sitting high in the midday sky. She felt hot and steamy inside her warm coat. She pulled it off carefully, not wanting to spook the gelding. Slowly he calmed down, and she leaned over to rub the white-lathered neck.

"Wish I could loosen the girth and let you breathe, old fellow, but you might take off without me." The prospect of being left alone on foot chilled her heart. Then she had an idea.

"On second thought, maybe you should take off

with me." She turned him around and, holding the reins as loosely as she dared, nudged him with her heels. "Come on, boy—you know the way home."

The gelding ambled this way and that through the forest. Skittish as he was, Hattie began to doubt his instincts. She looked up at the patches of sky peeking through the trees.

"Lord, You know the way home," she whispered. "Please show us, too."

They wandered perhaps a mile along the tangled path before Itchy's ears perked and his step grew more sure. Hattie worried about Colleen's silence, fervently hoping she hadn't caught up with the prowling panther. The gelding's nostrils flared as he suddenly nickered.

From somewhere through the trees came an answering neigh and a shrill whistle. Hattie couldn't whistle back, she was grinning so hard and felt such a flood of emotions.

"Over here!" she cried, urging Itchy to a trot.

Within moments both boys came to a stop beside her.

"What happened?" demanded Sam worriedly. He jumped down to check her, and then the gelding, carefully. "I thought you were back with Vince, and then all this screaming starts up ahead."

"He ran off and left me," said Hattie defensively. "So I tried to find you." She knew that wasn't exactly right, but catching Colleen by herself didn't seem like such a bright idea now.

Sam stared coldly at Vince. "Is that true?"

Vince shrugged, checking the knot in the rope he'd tied on Colleen. "When I looked around, she was gone."

Sam started to say something else, then shook his head and turned to Hattie. "Girl, you've scared me out of another year's growth. I take it you found the cat."

She nodded, and her eyes grew round. "It was the biggest, meanest-looking thing I've ever seen, Sam. And it was black. Have you ever seen a black one?"

"No, but I've heard tell of black panthers. Folks say they sometimes come up through Mexico."

"Did Colleen catch it?" Hattie wanted to know.

"She treed it and was bellowing loud enough for the county to hear when I found her," Sam said. "The panther was already gone though."

"How?" Hattie was mystified.

"The trees were real close together. I guess the brute climbed over to a tree hanging over the creek, then dropped down and swam off. Colleen couldn't find a scent."

"I didn't think cats liked water."

"This one's smart. He'll do whatever it takes to save his skin." Sam sighed and swung into the saddle. "And we've done all we can today too. Let's go home."

9

❖

Dark, Dark Clouds

The three rode home in silence. When the woods gave way to the Marshalls' lower pasture, Hattie called back to the boys, "Beat you to the barn!"

Sam waved her on. "Go see if dinner's ready. I need to talk to Vince a minute."

He's sounding more like Papa all the time, she thought. What could be more important than telling their story to the rest of the family? She left them in deep conversation and noticed Esther and Vashti grazing behind the split-rail fence. Both were heavy with calves, and Hattie was anxious for their arrival. She hoped at least one would look like its sire, the Shelleys' handsome Jersey bull. Even when mixed with the ancient longhorn blood, many of his offspring were golden, fawnlike beauties.

"Find any sign of the cat?" Papa asked as she rode up.

"We sure did," she exclaimed, and the story began to tumble out. When she finished, Papa shook his head.

83

"That's too close, Hattie Belle. Your Mama's going to skin me for letting you go, and she'll be right. Better get on in to dinner now."

As Papa unsaddled the gelding, Hattie walked stiffly to the house, knowing she'd feel bowlegged for the rest of the day. She sat on the porch to pry off the muddy boots and shake leaves from the cuffs of Sam's outgrown overalls.

"Quit dumping the swamp all over this porch," said Rosalie, coming out with the broom. Hattie ignored her and stood up to brush the gray, flannel shirt that swallowed any hint of femininity.

"Dinner ready? I'm starved."

"Almost. Don't come in till you've washed up."

"I'll be glad when you're bossing Lester around instead of us," said Hattie, glancing over at the barn. Sam had ridden in and was talking earnestly with Papa.

The panther was still the topic of conversation when they sat down to hot sourdough bread and chili. Hattie decided not to mention her personal encounter if Sam or Papa didn't. They were quiet.

"What if the cat's around when the new calves come?" she asked. "Will they be safe in the pasture?"

"They should be," said Mama. "Besides, can you imagine anything bothering Vashti's baby?"

"Well, if it's a girl, I'm going to find a way to gentle the calf." Hattie hoped both calves would be heifers so she could make pets of them. Male calves were raised for beef and weren't pets; getting attached was too painful.

"A heifer would probably be the best milk cow we've ever had," said Mama. "The Shelleys have more cream than they know what to do with. We might even have enough butter to sell."

Papa, usually enthusiastic about livestock, said nothing. Why was he so quiet today?

"Well, the Shelley cows are certainly better-looking than these old longhorns," said Rosalie.

Sam finally spoke up. "Looks aren't important when it comes to surviving drought and hard winters. A longhorn can eat scrub and walk a thousand miles and still have enough meat on his bones to fetch a fair price."

"With railroads going every which way, they won't have to walk much longer," said Mama. "They can buy a ticket."

Sam looked at Papa. "You're right, Mama—they won't have to walk much longer." He took a deep breath, then spoke quickly. "That's why I'm going this year."

"Going where?" asked Hattie, her spoon poised in midair.

"On a trail drive to Montana. Vince and me signed with a fellow named Taylor who's leaving with two hundred head next week. We'll join the main herd at Buffalo Springs."

Sam looked around the table to weigh the effect of his words. Despite his serious face, his blue-gray eyes glowed with excitement. Hattie sat in stunned silence, that morning's adventure forgotten.

Mama got up to clear the table without finishing her meal. She stopped next to Papa. "Andrew, you knew about this?" she demanded.

"Not until today." He patted her arm. "But we've talked, and I think it might be for the best, Alice. A young fellow should do something exciting before he settles down."

"Settles down" woke Hattie up. Lorene—somehow this must all be her fault.

"When will you get back?" asked Gramma, knowing there was no point in debate. She'd seen that look in men's eyes before.

"Before winter," said Sam.

"You won't be here for my wedding then," said Rosalie.

"No," he said slowly. "I'm sorry, Rose, but this is something I can't put off till next year." For once there was no teasing, no animosity between them.

Rosalie pondered Sam's words a moment. "Do you have plans for next year?"

"Could be." He pushed back from the table and relaxed a little. "But let's not get the plow before the mule. Anyhow, you don't want me around trying to talk sense into Lester, do you?"

Rosalie shook her head with an understanding smile.

Hattie, however, understood nothing except that

Sam was leaving her behind. Unable to speak, she flew out the door.

❖

"Hattie! C'mon, I know you're out here," called Sam. He had checked her red oak and the barn before searching the creek bank behind it, another of her favorite haunts. He found her slumped against a tree trunk, pretending not to hear. Quiet sniffles had given her away.

He sat beside her on the damp cushion of leaves. "Guess I should've told you sooner."

"Why didn't you?"

"Saw no reason to before we were sure about the drive."

"Lorene's got something to do with this, doesn't she?" she blurted, turning to him. "When were you going to tell me about *that*?"

Sam flinched at the hurt and anger in her face.

"Lorene's a wonderful girl," he said slowly. "Maybe she did turn my mind down a new road."

"Have you proposed?"

"No, and I won't till I'm sure it's right. The trouble is, I keep thinking about Papa."

"Well, if you're worried about him needing help, how can you just take off?"

"I don't mean the work. Whenever I get married, I'll probably stay right here. That's just it. Grandpa went to war leaving Papa saddled with a family when he wasn't much older than you. He's forty-three now and hasn't been farther than Galveston his whole life." Sam sighed and shook his head. "Hattie, I don't want to grow old without ever *doing* anything. Can't you see that now's the best time?"

Hattie's bottom lip trembled, and her chest felt so tight she could hardly breathe. "I don't know what I'll do without you."

He wrapped a long arm around her shoulders. "Oh, you'll stay plenty busy, and I'll be back before the trail's cold."

"No, you won't," she said, hot tears spilling down her cheeks. "Those drives are long and dangerous. Every day I'll worry and wonder about you, and it'll seem like forever. And when you come back . . . and get married . . . it won't . . ." She covered her face as great sobs broke loose.

Sam gently stroked her dark head. "It won't what?" he asked softly.

Hattie struggled to catch her breath. "It won't . . . be the same anymore."

They sat in silence awhile, hearing only the creek's whisper. He finally spoke. "You know, I was only seven when you were born, but I'll never forget that day. I wanted a brother so bad I could taste it, Rosalie being such a bother and all. When they said you were a girl, I was mighty disappointed.

"Then Gramma brought you out for me to hold. I'd never seen anything so pretty—like a little, pink rosebud. So we sat and rocked, and I thought maybe a sister would do if she was raised right. I started planning how I'd teach you to ride and climb and fish."

A tender smile crept across Sam as he wiped his sister's tear-stained face. "Looks like I did a good job."

Hattie thought back to the gangly boy in whose shadow she had taken her first steps. "I remember bawling on the porch when you'd leave for school."

"Yeah. I thought if you got loud enough, Mama would let me stay home," he said. "But she never did."

They both laughed a little. Then he lifted her face to look straight into his own.

"Hattie, some things have to change as we grow up. It's part of life and God's plan. But there are other things that won't ever change. Understand?"

She nodded, determined not to ever let him see her cry again.

The week passed swiftly as Sam got his gear in shape and packed the few personal belongings he could carry with him. Mama seemed determined to send along enough food to last the whole trip.

"A cowpoke's not supposed to get fat on the trail," he teased as she took inventory.

"I'm sure you boys won't let it go to waste."

"No, ma'am. Vince's ma has the same idea though."

"When will he be ready?" asked Mama.

"Sunup tomorrow. He's making the rounds today telling everyone bye." Sam finished oiling the new cowhide boots Papa had insisted on buying, saying the old pair wouldn't make it to the Panhandle.

"Don't forget to pick up the parcel Mrs. Conroy wanted taken to her daughter in Fort Worth."

"I'll stop by on the way to Doc's. Why can't she mail it?"

"It's something she made for the new grandbaby, and she won't trust it with the mail."

"Oh. Well, I hope it's not something heavy or bulky like a quilt."

Mama noticed Hattie dawdling over her grits. "Time for school," she said.

"Can't I go with Sam today? Please?"

"No, Hattie. He has things to do. Now find your slicker and get along."

"I don't know where it is." She picked up her lunch pail as if thunder clouds were sitting on her shoulders. "It's not going to rain anyway."

"I'll be home early," said Sam. "You can help me get Chica ready."

She nodded and disappeared into the gray morning. *Maybe the weather will get worse*, she thought, *and they'll have to put off leaving.*

School seemed long and meaningless that day. She stared out the window at the heavy skies, hoping they would drop a deluge and make the dirt roads useless. If the local herd couldn't leave in time to join the large one, perhaps they would forget the whole thing. Just maybe . . . *Please, Lord*, she prayed, *make it rain hard.*

"Hattie, are you not feeling well today?" asked Miss Kate.

"No, ma'am . . . I mean, yes, ma'am."

"Then may I see what you've written?"

Hattie stared at her blank slate. "I'm sorry. What was the question?"

Miss Kate sighed and called on Eric. *Of course he knows the worst plagues of the ancient world*, Hattie nearly said aloud. *His father's a doctor and his precious cousin almost a nurse.* She thought of Sam telling Lorene good-bye and fought the jealousy that knotted her stomach. No one could possibly miss him as much as she would. Well, if it rained enough maybe he wouldn't go and she wouldn't have to miss him at all.

A drizzle began as school ended, and Miss Kate loaded her buggy with children. "Hop in, Hattie," she said.

Hattie shook her head. "Where are you going?" she asked Rosalie.

"The store. Lester's mother has new piece goods in that she wants me to see. He'll bring me home later," said Rosalie. "You'd better go with Miss Kate. Mama wouldn't want you out in the weather."

"I don't mind. It's just a sprinkle," said Hattie over her shoulder. It was a thirty-minute walk, but riding Miss Kate's route would take more than an hour by the time she dropped off the other children. Hattie was too anxious to get home, even if it meant getting wet.

Soon she had left town behind and was tromping

briskly down the narrow logging road toward home. The wind picked up, whistling between tall stands of pine on either side and pelting her with bits of sleet. Maybe this hadn't been such a good idea after all.

She tied on her bonnet and turned hopefully at the sound of hoofbeats.

"Hey, knothead, are you wet enough?" came Vince's voice from beneath his slicker.

"Oh, it's you."

"That's no way to greet your ride home." He offered a hand.

She hadn't talked to him since Sam announced their plans, and she wasn't in the mood to do so now. Still, the sleet was coming down harder . . . She took his hand and was hoisted onto the horse's slick rump, holding tightly to the saddle as they trotted on.

"Sure hope this weather clears before tomorrow," he said.

"What if it doesn't?" asked Hattie. "Maybe the roads will wash out and the drive will get canceled."

"Not likely. Carl Taylor has too much invested in those cows not to go. Besides, the trail boss is a friend of his. They'll wait."

Vince glanced back as her face fell. "I take it you're not pleased about us going."

"Go anywhere you like," she snapped. "Just leave Sam out of it."

"Ain't that a mite selfish?"

The anger and hurt she had fought all week finally exploded. "Me? You're the one too yellow to do anything on your own, so you drag him along!"

She reached around him, yanking the reins. "Let me off this nag!"

Vince watched in amazement as she slid down onto the ice-peppered road. The sleet had turned into small hailstones, which Hattie fended off with her coat as she made long strides toward home.

"Are you crazy?" he yelled above the storm. "I can have you at the house in five minutes."

"Leave me alone!" she cried. "Better yet, leave Sam alone!"

Vince pulled his mare in front of her. "Your ma would skin me if I left you out here. Now climb on!"

"I'd rather walk all the way to China!" Hattie scooped up a handful of muddy ice and drew back her throwing arm.

Vince shook his head. "I hope you grow up some before we get back," he shouted.

She flung the glob of red mud and ice. He ducked, but it caught the back of his head, splattering down his slicker.

"I hope you get lost and never come back!" she screamed into the wind.

Vince McKinney galloped off toward the sawmill, hesitating a moment as he passed the Marshall farm.

Some time later, soaked and stinging from the ice, Hattie stumbled onto the porch.

10

❖

Fritters

Hattie Belle!" Mama looked in dismay at her dripping daughter standing in the doorway. "I thought Miss Kate would drop you off."

"It was hardly raining when I left school," Hattie chattered, pulling off her outer garments by the fire. She decided the ride she *did* have wasn't worth mentioning.

"All we need is for you to get sick again," fussed Gramma. "Change quick now, and dry that hair."

"I'm all right, Gramma. Is Sam back?"

"He's in the barn."

The men soon came in for the feast prepared for Sam's going away. Not that Mama considered it a cause to celebrate, but she knew how long it would be before she cooked for her son again. Even in Hattie's somber mood, the chicken and dumplings had never tasted better than after that cold walk home.

"Um-m-m, Mama, this is the best," Sam said

with a smile. "Wish there was a way to pack dumplings."

"You'll be stopping in towns along the way," said Rosalie. "There should be places to eat and shop."

"Hope so," he said, dishing up seconds. "What can I bring you back?"

She pondered. "Well . . . maybe something for my new house."

"What about you, Gramma?" he asked cheerily.

"I don't need anything, dear."

"Mama?"

Mama didn't have to think. "Just you home safe."

"All right. Hattie, how about you?"

She thought a moment, silently agreeing with Mama. "An Indian necklace, if you see one."

"I'll keep my eyes peeled. Papa, is there something in Colorado you've hankered for?"

"A nugget from one of those gold mines would come in handy." Papa chuckled. He was excited for Sam now, as if the adventure were partly his. "Better yet, while you're in the Rockies, find one of those photographer fellers and have your picture made. It'll be a good keepsake."

"I'll try." Sam pushed his chair back. "Ladies, I won't have another meal like this for at least six months. But any more and I'll colic and have to stay home." He stood up to stretch his muscles.

"Hattie, grab a coat. I've got something to show you."

She followed him to the barn, knowing the twinkle in his eyes meant something special. He opened the barn door, hung the lantern, and knelt down in an empty stall. Peeking over his shoulder, she caught her breath.

"Oh, Sam!" She watched in disbelief as a ball of curly, black fur unrolled and stretched, its pink mouth open in a wide yawn. The puppy wiggled to its feet and stared back at her with brown button eyes. Irresistibly she touched the velvety head and soft, floppy ears. "Where did it come from?"

"Conroys. Saw the litter when I picked up that parcel. Mrs. Conroy wanted to pay me for taking the package for her, but I asked for this little fellow instead. His mama's some kind of retriever. Mr. Conroy hunts ducks with her—says she's as sharp as they come."

Hattie cradled the black bundle in her lap as he nibbled her thumb. She noticed the narrow, white stripe that ran from chest to stomach in sharp contrast to the inky coat. "He's so beautiful," she whispered. "What are you going to call him?"

"He's not mine to name. What can *you* think of?"

Looking into her brother's kind, blue eyes, she realized that Sam was doing all he could to ease the pain of his leaving. "I don't know what fits him yet," she said.

"Well, you can write and tell me."

She was puzzled. "How? I don't know where you'll be."

"Mama has a list of towns we should pass through. I'll check the post office in every one."

"All right then," she said. "Will you write me too?"

"Every chance I get," he promised.

❖

Mama was up at 4 the next morning cooking apple fritters. Hattie amazed her by stumbling into the kitchen to help. She couldn't sleep anyway. Late into the night she had tossed and turned, counting the dangers of the trail—bandits, floods, rattlers, stampedes—one for nearly each letter of the alphabet. When she did doze off, some vague, awful dream had jolted her back to the shadowy reality of her room.

She yawned at Mama. "How much cinnamon?"

"A pinch. When that's mixed, put the apples in."

Mama checked the skillet of grease, which already smelled hot. When the grease started to move around, she carefully dropped in a spoonful of batter. It sizzled and spat as the pastry swelled up and turned golden brown on the bottom. She turned it with a fork and went to check the coffee.

"I can do it now," said Hattie.

"All right, but watch that grease. You're half asleep."

Hattie tried to spoon the dough in just like Mama had done, though the shapes were altogether different. She decided Sam should have the biggest and best of all, so she plopped in enough dough to fill half the skillet. She watched as it grew the size of the pan. The grease was hotter now, so the huge fritter browned quickly.

"I wouldn't make them all that big," warned Mama.

"I'm not," she replied, quickly spooning in the remaining dough. The others were small, and they almost burned before she could turn them. Some things were not as easy as they looked.

As the men poured their coffee and sat down to breakfast, Hattie proudly served the pile of odd-shaped pastries. Sam stared at the fritter that covered his plate.

"That would fill a bear," said Papa.

Mama shot him a warning look. "Hattie helped cook this morning."

"And it looks terrific," said Sam, digging in cheerfully.

Hattie wasn't hungry, but she found satisfaction in watching her brother enjoy the fruit of her labors. He paused when he got to the fritter's middle and long strings of dough clung to his fork.

"It's raw," she moaned.

"It's fine," he insisted, wolfing down the rest between gulps of coffee. "Can we pack what's left? They'll be good on the trail."

"For feeding buzzards," mumbled Hattie. She shoved a small, tough pastry into her pocket for the pup. *They like chewy things*, she thought.

They heard Vince's horse outside, so Sam said good-bye to Gramma, who couldn't manage the steps yet. Everyone else followed him outside, even a bleary-eyed Rosalie in her dressing gown. There was much hugging and last-minute advice. Hattie coldly ignored Vince until he stepped in front of her.

"Aren't you going to tell me a proper good-bye?" he asked, more earnest than usual. "In case I get lost?"

Hattie set her jaw and looked him square in the eyes. "Don't you come back without Sam," she warned.

Then it was time. The black pup pulled at her shoes as Sam wrapped Hattie in a bear hug. All the parting words Hattie had thought up last night escaped her now as she clung to him. Then he knelt to pull Hattie's laces from the pup's tiny teeth and handed him to her.

"This fellow will be nearly grown by the time I get back. Keep him out of trouble. And both of you stay out of the woods. Can't have you running into that cat again, you know."

She nodded. With a quick peck on her forehead, he swung onto Chica and took a last, long look around. He sighed, and his sad expression puzzled her. Wasn't this what he wanted?

Then the shadow passed. He smiled, tipped his hat to them all, and vanished into the gray morning mist.

Silence filled the yard. Hattie couldn't move or

cry or say anything for a moment. She felt hollow inside, like an empty eggshell ready to crumble at the slightest touch.

Papa cleared his throat. "Better feed your young'un and get ready for school," he said gently.

She remembered the apple fritter in her pocket. The pup eagerly pulled it from her, his ears flopping.

"Glad it's good for something," she whispered as she took him to the barn. She pictured Sam choking down the last crumb of his awful breakfast. *It's amazing what love will do*, she thought.

After fixing the pup a bed of clean straw, she leaned back and closed weary eyes as the hot tears finally escaped.

"Please keep him safe, Father," she prayed. "Please, please bring him home safe."

Hours later the puppy's pink tongue woke Hattie, wrapped snug in the quilt Mama had brought from the house.

11

Blackberry Baby

Dear Sam,

    I named the pup Fritter. He likes my cooking better than anyone else does. I'll practice for when you get home.

    How does Chica like driving so many cows? Hope the rivers you crossed weren't flooded. What did you see in Fort Worth? Please write when you can. I can't wait to hear about it all.

    Everyone here is okay. Gramma moves slowly with her cane, but she gets around. Papa has started the spring plowing, and the fruit trees are in bloom. Ida gave Rosalie a party for her seventeenth birthday. Now all she does is plan for the wedding. I'll be glad when it's over.

    Esther had a boy calf. It's a red roan like her. I was disappointed.

    That panther got into the McKinneys' chicken house and killed four hens. All they found were the cat's tracks.

I miss you something awful. Be careful.
Love,
Hattie

Hattie carefully folded her letter and slipped it into the envelope with Mama's. Then she went outside. It was a gorgeous day. Spring had burst forth suddenly, and nature was in perfect unison. The clear air was filled with the sweet perfume of wisteria and the chatter of birds repairing last year's nests.

Through the woods she could see dogwood scattered like white beacons and taller trees proudly waving their fresh baby leaves as though they were celebrating being alive all over again. Spring usually made Hattie feel the same way, but her heart was far too heavy now. She wondered if it would ever feel light again.

Her thoughts were interrupted by Fritter's sharp puppy bark. "What's he into now?" she muttered.

She followed the sound around the barn but stopped suddenly when she saw Fritter standing in the cow lot, yapping at a furious Vashti. The cow's head was low, the wide, hooked horns level with the puppy as she pawed the ground.

"Fritter! Come here!" Hattie shouted as she clapped her hands. The dog looked back but was having too much fun to listen. Hattie grabbed the long pole she used to herd the cows, but just then Vashti bellowed and charged the pup. He suddenly realized this was no longer a game and scurried toward Hattie.

She knew he wouldn't make it in time, so she jumped onto the rail fence. She hurled the pole, spearlike, at the angry cow. It fell short and bounced into Vashti's face. She veered off as the black ball of fur dashed under the fence. Hattie scooped him up.

"You crazy pup," she scolded. "Don't you know when a cow is *serious*?"

He licked her face, trembling all over. In the short time since Sam had left, Fritter had grown much bigger and bolder. *Too bold*, she thought as she kept an eye on Vashti. He'd have to be penned up when the calf came, or he'd get stomped for sure.

"Wait a minute," said Hattie. "That cow's not as big as she was when I milked her this morning. And where's she headed now?"

Hattie locked Fritter in the barn and sprinted across the pasture. In the back a thicket of blackberry vines had grown around an old tree stump. The ground dropped sharply behind it, and into that tangle Vashti had disappeared. Hattie quietly climbed the stump to get a better look.

Nestled among the stickers with their tiny, white blooms lay a small, golden bundle. Vashti, a blackberry vine dangling from one horn, licked it tenderly.

Hattie smiled. A baby couldn't have a more doting mama, but heaven help the rest of them.

Well, she thought, *is it a boy or a girl?* She pondered on how to find out without upsetting Vashti, then ran to the barn. She returned with a bucket of cracked corn, shook it noisily, and called, "Hoo-ee, come on, cow . . ."

Vashti's bony head peeked from behind the thicket. Esther mooed from the small pen, and Hattie gave her a bite. That did it. Vashti trotted up, complaining all the way. Hattie waited until the cow's face was buried in the bucket, then hurried around to the back of the field, entering the thicket from behind. Dodging the stickers, she tiptoed in. The calf looked at her with huge, liquid-brown eyes and twitched its wet, black nose.

"Hello, baby," Hattie cooed. "You're a pretty thing." She stroked the soft, damp hair.

The calf sniffed her, not knowing to be afraid.

"That's right—I'm your friend. No matter what your mama says."

Hattie looked the calf over thoroughly.

"You're a girl!" she cried, hugging the startled heifer. Just then the bushes moved violently.

"Uh-oh . . ." said Hattie, turning to face an angry Vashti. Why hadn't she brought the pole? Though she and the cows certainly shared a mutual respect, Hattie had never been afraid of a cow—until now. She backed away from the calf as Vashti bellowed, charging through the vines.

Hattie looked at the great stump above. The ground had washed out badly on the lower side, leaving old roots exposed. She didn't know if it would hold her, but she jumped anyway, grabbing a large root. The stump shook, showering her with dirt as she began to pull herself up. Something hard sent a sharp pain through her leg.

She looked down at Vashti's long horns, twisting to catch her again. Almost without thinking about it, she put one foot on the cow's bony forehead and pulled herself up again. Vashti tossed her head, giving Hattie just the boost she needed. Hattie cleared the embankment with a *thump* and ran limping to the house.

"Mama, Papa—it's a heifer! She's beautiful."

P.S. Sam, guess what? Vashti had a Jersey heifer. We named her Beauty. She already likes me. Vashti doesn't like anyone right now. She ran me out of the blackberry thicket. Wish you had been here.

In the following weeks corn, cotton, and peas were sown in the large fields near the woods. A smaller patch of vegetables that required more care was planted near the creek. This garden, Mama's domain, was protected from chickens and varmints by a tall picket fence.

"Hattie, what's that pup doing in here?" Mama fussed one day. "He'll dig up everything he doesn't trample."

"I don't know," said Hattie, her nimble fingers tying bean vines onto pole tepees. "I shut the gate and told him to wait outside."

"Well, he wants to be with you," Mama added. "Put him someplace where he can't get out till Papa can fix the fence. He'll be back from town soon."

"He'll soon be too big to squeeze through," said Hattie, grunting as she picked up Fritter.

"When he's bigger, he'd better mind."

Hattie wiped the dark garden soil from Fritter's feet that looked three sizes too large, then took him to the house.

"Don't bring that smelly pup in here," protested Rosalie.

"Mama said to put him up, and he cries in the barn."

"You're going to have him so spoiled that he'll expect to eat at the table next."

"Good idea," said Hattie. "He can have your place when you're gone." She dodged a flying dish-towel and ambled back to the garden.

With the wedding only weeks away, Hattie was thinking hard about what life would be like after-wards. Sam's leaving had not only torn a piece of her heart away—it had meant more chores. Papa wasn't trying to burden her; he just needed an extra pair of hands. Of course, she didn't really mind outside chores, but what would Rosalie's absence mean? She was always cooking, sewing, or scrubbing something. Hattie had no desire to fill those dainty shoes.

The beans were tied and grass pulled when Hattie and her mother heard Papa's horse. They raised up stiffly and called to him, "Any mail?"

His broad smile answered their question as he waved the saddlebag. Hattie darted through the gate and grabbed the fat leather pouch.

"Clean your hands first," said Mama, washing hers at the pump. But Hattie couldn't wait.

"It's here!" She waved a worn envelope. "Just for me."

"There's another one for all of us," chuckled Papa. He handed a larger envelope to Mama, who took it as eagerly as Hattie.

"It was mailed from Doan's Crossing—where's that, Papa?"

"Near the Panhandle, I think. You can check the map Miss Kate gave you. They should be in Colorado by now."

"Gramma and Rosalie should hear this." Mama looked back at Hattie. "Come on. We need you, too."

Hattie opened the envelope addressed to her, then hesitated. "I'll be there in a minute," she mumbled. When they had gone into the house, she ran to the red oak and, tucking the letter in her pocket, climbed to her perch. There she propped just right and carefully opened the thin, smudged sheets of paper. Tears blurred her vision as she read the familiar script.

Dear Hattie,

Just arrived at Doan's Crossing on the Red River and was pleased to find news from home. Glad the mail moves faster than these cows—nearly 3,000 of them. There are 15 men including the cook, and 69 horses. Chica is fine. I save her for riding night herd on account of her good eyes and sense. She hasn't liked water since that day on the Sabine, and I had a time getting her across the Trinity. The herd was a sight—a river full of horns and noses.

That was nothing compared to the storm that hit us on the prairie. You've never seen such lightning. It scattered and ran across the ground like blue fire. The tips of the cows' horns glowed, and they got mighty nervous. We kept them in a mill (that's a tight circle) until it was over. The next night they did stampede when we ran across a herd of javelinas. Took hours to round them up.

Vince and me are riding flank, which is no great honor. Still, it beats riding tail where you eat 4 lbs. of dust a day. That's for the real greenhorns. Vince says howdy and that he's not lost yet.

So far the trail is all we hoped it would be. This country is amazing, and we're not even to the mountains yet. I've never seen so many stars at night or birds in the daytime. Huge flocks stop to feed after we've passed, and the wildflowers go on and on.

Wish you were here to see it all. Maybe Mama will let me bring you on the train someday. We'll work on it. Give them all my best. Watch it around those cows, and keep old Fritter out of trouble. It's a good name.

I love you very much.

Sam

12

❖

The Blue Silk Dress

"**H**ello, babies," Hattie cooed as she slipped into the calf pen. Now that Papa had separated the two calves from the cows during the day, she had a chance of gentling the golden heifer. "Come here, Beauty—I won't hurt you."

She held out a handful of salt, which the calf licked eagerly. The great brown eyes suspiciously watched the rope halter in Hattie's other hand. Slowly Hattie rubbed it against the calf's soft neck, then moved up to scratch the doelike ears.

"Hattie!" Rosalie shouted from the porch.

"Not now," she muttered.

"Will you get in here?"

The calf pulled away, and Hattie sighed with disappointment.

"What do you want?" she yelled, leaving the cow pen and stomping into the house.

"You have to try on this dress before I can finish it," said Rosalie. "Phew! You smell like one of those calves. Go wash before you put it on."

"I'm fine," grumbled Hattie, grabbing the pale blue silk dress and slipping it over her head.

"Ouch! Help me—I'm stuck."

Rosalie removed a pin and pulled the dress into place.

"I can't breathe," said Hattie, plucking at the high gathered collar. "And it's too long."

"You should have put the bustle and petticoat on first." Rosalie handed her a white bundle. "They'll take up the length."

Hattie's eyes grew wide as she stared at the stiff, white taffeta. Had the Christmas present she buried in the pasture last month come back to haunt her?

"Where did you get that?" she whispered.

"I had to borrow them since yours *disappeared*."

"Oh." Hattie sighed with relief. "Well, you can give 'em back." She tossed the undergarments on the bed.

"The dress won't look right without them."

Hattie squared her jaw. "I don't care. Just look at these sleeves. They're as big as loaves of bread."

"Full sleeves are the rage now. You'll look fashionable."

"I'll look stupid," said Hattie, struggling out of the dress.

Rosalie stood as straight as she could, hands on hips. "Hattie Marshall, you're just plain ornery. This wedding is the most important thing that's ever happened to me, so stop trying to spoil it."

"Well, I didn't ask to be a bridesmaid and wear

this thing in front of everyone," snapped Hattie. "Why don't you ask Ida Shelley? She'd love to do it."

For a moment Hattie couldn't tell if her sister looked more mad or hurt. Rosalie stared at the blue dress as her mouth grew white around tight lips. "All right, if you don't want to . . . I'll ask Ida today," she said, slamming the door behind her.

Hattie heard Mama's voice on the porch. "Rosalie, what do you mean Hattie's not going to stand with you? She's your only sister."

"Well, she doesn't want to, and that's fine with me."

"I'm afraid you're both going to regret this," said Mama.

Part of Hattie already did. The other part felt like a fish that had just wiggled its way off a hook.

The girls had little to say as the days flew by. Hattie was busy with the gardens, while Mama and the other women cooked and cleaned for the wedding. Many trips were made to consult with Mrs. Forbes and get the apartment over the store ready for the newlyweds.

Mama spent hours altering the ivory-colored, satin dress that had been her mother's, the very dress she had worn at her own wedding. Rosalie was close enough to the same size to use it, and she felt very honored to do so. This concerned Mrs. Forbes, who had a pattern for a fine, new gown. Still, Rosalie insisted on wearing Grandma Pruitt's dress.

Lester's mother seemed relieved—and surprised—when she saw the beautiful old gown and a small daguerreotype of Mama's parents at their elegant Savannah wedding. "Even farm folk can have nice things," was Mama's only comment.

At last the day arrived. The Louisiana cousins had come earlier in the week, and Hattie was amazed at how the baby had grown. Had it been only eight months since that trip? Enough had happened to fill two years.

Now the little one was crawling everywhere, an accident waiting to happen. The four-year-old twins were just as much trouble, usually either meddling or chasing Fritter. Hattie complained to Mama about the situation.

"Don't be such a mother hen, Hattie. That pup's as rowdy as they are, and he loves the attention."

She knew it was probably true, for at six months her "baby" was a forty-pound explosion of energy. If they just wouldn't pull his ears . . .

Still, she preferred chasing little ones to doing kitchen duty. Mama, Gramma, and Aunt Millie had baked until they declared the stove was tired. Counting themselves, friends, and the Forbes family, Mama expected to feed nearly a hundred people. Papa and Uncle Burl had set up long plank tables on the side of the house away from the chicken yard. Two live oaks locked branches there to provide inviting shade. Grandpa Marshall had planted those trees when his children were born. Papa followed the tradition, and three smaller trees stood nearby.

Rosalie had picked the spot in early spring and had planted flower beds around the trees. Colorful verbena, Indian blanket, and bluebells waved in the magnolia-sweet breeze.

The guests arrived late that morning. Many brought their favorite recipes, as well as gifts for the couple. Soon the yard was filled with wagons, buggies, and the happy chatter of people glad for a reason to celebrate. Hattie enjoyed the company and, even more, the chance to show Fritter off—at least, until Mama found her.

"You'd better get dressed," Mama said. "It's almost time."

Hattie followed her to the house and stopped short when she opened the bedroom door. Rosalie and Ida had been holed up there all morning. She'd never seen so many hairpins and clothes or so much makeup strewn in one place. *Miss Nitpick must have lost control*, she thought, shaking her head.

Then she noticed a third figure in the corner and stiffened. It was indeed Hattie's bedroom, but she would have been more comfortable stepping off a boat in China.

"Lorene's fixing my bouquet," said Rosalie, arranging her curls. "Isn't it lovely?"

"I guess," mumbled Hattie. She had avoided

talking to Lorene since Sam left, and she didn't care to speak with her now.

"It's a bit crowded in here," said Lorene. "I can do this elsewhere." She gathered a basket of jasmine and tea roses.

"No need," said Mama, finding Hattie's best shoes and stockings. "We'll change in my room."

Hattie followed her mother down the hall, concerned by the serious look on her face. When they reached Mama's room, she saw the reason. A familiar bundle of pale blue silk lay on the bed.

"Mama . . ."

"This dress is too pretty not to wear, young lady," said Mama in her voice that meant business. "I've made some changes so you'll be more comfortable in it."

"But, Mama . . ."

"No buts." Then Mama's face softened as she sat on the bed.

"Hattie Belle, this is Rosalie's day. Next to the day she accepted Jesus as her Savior, it's the most important day of her life. Don't be upset with her wanting everything just right. You'll understand better when it's your turn. But for now I want you to cooperate so we'll have good memories."

"My turn? I'm not getting married."

A smile flickered across Mama's face as she patted Hattie's hand. "We'll see. Now put on your petticoat. It's getting late."

Hattie looked around for the bustle Rosalie had borrowed.

Mama must have read her mind. "I cut the back of the skirt even with the front so it doesn't need the you-know-what."

Hattie gave a long sigh of relief. Mama was quiet as Hattie slipped on the petticoat and dress. She plucked at the ruffled sleeves, which didn't seem as full as before. It was like a different dress. She turned slowly in front of Mama's mirror. The new neckline scooped gently, and the silky material draped in soft folds from her narrow waist. The clothes she had grown up in were made of sturdy, homespun fabric or cotton prints. Nothing had ever felt like this.

"We don't have time to curl your hair, but we can put it in a twist." Mama quickly brushed the dark brown mane that hung nearly to Hattie's waist, then twisted it and pinned it in a neat ball at the base of her neck. After fastening a blue satin bow to it, Mama was finished.

"What do you think?" she asked.

Hattie stared at her reflection. It was like looking at a stranger—an older and much prettier stranger.

She turned a solemn face to Mama. "I don't look like me."

Mama's eyes grew misty, and she laughed—a soft, gentle laugh. "Go show your sister."

13

❖

The Wedding

Hattie found Rosalie and Ida still doing their hair. They stared in amazement. "Why, Hattie . . . you look sixteen."

Hattie wasn't sure how she felt about that.

"The dress is still nice, even with Mama's alterations. I wasn't sure . . ." Rosalie sighed. "Will you stand with me now?"

"But Ida's ready to . . ."

"Who says I can't have *two* bridesmaids?"

Hattie's eyes hurt for a moment, and she couldn't speak. Then for the first time since she came home from the river, she wrapped long, brown arms around her tiny sister. What was the house going to be like without her? She was surprised at her own feelings.

"Oh, I almost forgot," said Hattie, "Sam left something for me to give you today." She pulled a shiny, copper coin from her drawer. "You're supposed to have a penny in your shoe for luck."

Rosalie took it with a smile.

"It doesn't seem right, him not being here," said Hattie.

"I know," said Rosalie, "but he might have missed out on his dream waiting around for mine."

The thin strains of Uncle Burl's violin wafted through the window. "He's warming up," warned Ida. "We'd better finish your hair."

Outside a shout went up as Lester arrived with his mother in their black and red surrey. At that moment Mama and Lorene appeared at the bedroom door with the sweet-smelling bouquet.

When everyone was in place outside, Ida marched slowly down the steps. Hattie was supposed to follow and felt a moment of panic. The dress was longer than she was used to—what if she tripped and wound bottom-side-up on the ground? To keep from looking at the upturned faces of the crowd, she watched the steps, taking each with utmost care. From there she walked with all the dignity she could muster to stand near Ida. She sighed with relief once her procession was finished.

It was Rosalie's turn to walk down with Papa, who was tall and dignified-looking in his black suit. Hattie watched in awe when her sister descended the stairs of their log home as if she were a princess being wed in some great cathedral. The strawberry curls were combed out to float about her face, held by a band of tiny, white flowers. The long satin-and-lace gown embraced the top of her tiny form, while the skirt poufed out over the old-fashioned hoops. Hattie was amazed at the similarity between Rosalie and the picture of Grandma Pruitt. Could Mama have looked this way before all the babies and hard work?

Hattie watched her mother, whose eyes glistened with unshed tears. Gramma smiled; her joy at just being there was shared by all. Lorene sat beside her, to Hattie's dismay. *Already trying to act like one of the family*, she thought bitterly. *Sam might be here if it wasn't for her.*

Then Rosalie came forward to take Lester's arm. *Poor Lester*, thought Hattie. He was all spiffed up to perfection and sweating like a field hand. But he'd never worked in a field, and now Rosalie wouldn't have to. However things might change at home, Hattie was pleased that Rosalie was finding the kind of life she'd wanted.

Hattie tried unsuccessfully to listen as the preacher had Lester and Rosalie promise to do all sorts of things. But "as long as ye both shall live" kept ringing in her ears. *That's a long time.* She couldn't imagine wanting to be around any of the boys she knew that long. She figured she just wouldn't get married at all.

Suddenly the ceremony was over. Everyone stood and cheered as Rosalie turned to throw her bouquet—straight back to Lorene. Hattie groaned, then was besieged by hugs and pats on the back. It took a while for Mrs. Forbes's photographer to line up both families. Hattie was puzzled as to why everyone looked serious for the camera when they had been laughing just moments before. Yet as the Marshalls' turn came she felt a bit somber herself, wishing that *all* the family could be there.

Just then one of the twins pulled the other's hair, who screeched and whacked his brother. Everyone laughed as the camera *poufed*—everyone except Aunt Millie, who was trying to pull them apart. Hattie wondered how her red face would look in the black-and-white photograph.

The picture-taking over, friends and family lined up at the tables, heaping their plates with food of every sort. Hattie had just realized she was starved when Mama summoned her to serve lemonade.

"I'll mess up my dress," she protested.

"Just be careful," said Mama in a rush. "Don't stand too close."

The cold lemonade was going fast as the thirsty guests passed. Hattie was about to pour a full dipper into a glass when the unthinkable happened—someone bumped her elbow from behind.

"Oh!" The lemonade splashed down the front of her dress, soaking through the blue silk all the way to her skin. She stared in dismay.

"What?" said a gravelly voice. It was Doctor Siegen. "My dear, I am most sorry. Please . . ." He fumbled in his pockets for a handkerchief. "Please forgive my clumsiness."

"It's okay," mumbled Hattie. She rubbed the dress with the handkerchief, but it didn't help.

"No, it is *not* okay. I have ruined your lovely dress

and perhaps your afternoon as well. Please allow me to serve while you change," he said with a dignified bow.

Hattie almost giggled. He was sincere, and the dress *was* cold and sticky. "Well, all right. Thanks, Dr. Siegen. I'll hurry."

"I don't care who dips it. My gullet's drier than dust," complained Uncle Burl as the doc took up Hattie's post. She hurried to the house with the handkerchief in front of her, hoping to get by without anyone noticing.

But Mrs. McKinney blocked her way at the steps. "Hattie Belle, you look mighty fetching in that get-up. Like a regular young lady. Won't be surprised if one of my boys doesn't take notice and come calling."

Hattie's eyes widened as she shook her head. "I hope not."

Mrs. McKinney's hearty laugh followed her as Aunt Millie added, "I'll have to ask Alice what she's feeding that girl. She's shot up like a long-stemmed rose."

Dodging among the guests, Hattie finally made it to her room and slammed the door in relief. She looked at the mirror's reflection of the dark, wet silk. Her eyes filled with tears as she began to unbutton the dress.

"Quit that," she said to herself, angrily wiping the tears away. "It's just a stupid dress." But pulling on her blue gingham church dress, she had to admit that looking special had been nice—even for a little while.

She returned to the table to find the doctor enjoying his role as Master of Lemonade. He knew almost everyone, and the line moved slowly. Hattie never realized her neighbors had so many ailments.

"I can do this if you'd like to eat now," she said.

"Almost done. Here, hand me those glasses." He leaned over to whisper, "Do not ask Mrs. Conroy how she feels today. It would take until supper."

Hattie grinned. When everyone was served, including Mrs. Conroy, she followed him down the food line.

"Your mother's dumplings are gone," he said sadly. "And the peach pie."

"They never last long," said Hattie, stabbing a chicken leg. She looked around for a place to sit. Others were finishing as Uncle Burl warmed up his violin.

The doctor motioned to a bench under the oaks. "Since we are last, will you join me?"

They munched in silence, watching children dart about while the women picked up dishes and men lit their pipes. The younger people laughed and teased as they paired off to dance. Finally the doctor took a deep breath and rubbed his stomach.

"A lovely wedding, good food, pleasant company . . . an excellent day, yes?"

"I guess," said Hattie.

"You are sad about your dress. I forgot," he said. "Again, I am sorry."

"It's not that," she said quietly. "Not really. I just wish Sam was here."

"Ah." The doctor rubbed his chin. "He is missed in our home as well. Sam is a fine young man—and a good brother, I think."

"He's more than that," she insisted. "He's my best friend in the whole world."

"Then you are fortunate to have both. I have a brother, but as boys all we did was quarrel." He chuckled and shook his head. "Sometimes we quarreled so much, the furniture broke. Now that we have grown more sense, he lives far away."

"Where's that?"

"New York."

Hattie sighed. "Sometimes I'm afraid Sam won't come back. Anything could happen out there in the wilderness, or he might just like it better there and decide to stay."

Doctor Siegen squeezed her hand gently. "Hattie, you must trust God, who loves him as much as you do and who placed in our hearts a compass that always points home."

The tears Hattie had fought throughout the wedding now spilled down her cheeks. Not wanting the doctor to see, she looked away toward the trees Papa had planted when she and Sam and Rosalie were born.

"Why do we have to grow up anyway?" she whispered, half to herself. "Everything was fine before. Now it's all turned upside-down."

"Change comes harder for some of us, I think,"

said the doctor. "Yet we must not be afraid but must rather look for the good things ahead. The Father has promised many blessings to His children, you know."

Hattie wiped her face and nodded. "Gramma says that, too. I guess she's lived long enough to know."

He laughed. "That grandmother of yours knows a great deal—except how to be a good patient."

Hattie had to laugh at that. Just then Lorene and Eric found them.

"Uncle Josef, this boy refuses to dance with me anymore. Have you taught him this?"

"Certainly not." The physician stood with effort, bowed, and offered Lorene an arm. "May I redeem the name of Siegen?"

With that, they joined the circle and were whisked away in a flurry of music and long, ruffled skirts. Eric fidgeted, running his hands through neatly cropped blond hair. It was straight and wispy like his mother's, while his eyebrows were heavy and a shade darker, so that he always looked like he was thinking hard.

Uncle Burl's lively tune suddenly picked up the pace. "All join hands . . ."

There was a long, miserable silence as Hattie wished Eric would go away and leave her alone with her red eyes and dreary mood. Instead, he drew in the dust with his shiny, black shoes.

"I don't suppose . . ." he mumbled, "that you'd want to . . . I mean, you might, but not with me . . ."

His face turned pink. "Do you want to dance?" he said in a rush.

Hattie's eyes widened as she shook her head. "No indeed."

"Well, that's a relief!" He sank to the bench and loosened his tie. "Lorene said you probably did."

"What!" Hattie jumped up. "I most certainly do not. Why can't she mind her own business?"

Eric was startled. "I don't think she meant . . ." he stammered. "It's just her way . . . trying to figure out what other people are feeling. I guess it's part of being a nurse."

Hattie sat down, still flustered.

Eric changed the subject. "What are you doing now that school's out?"

She shrugged, still fuming over Lorene's trying to embarrass her. "Working the garden mostly. This is a farm, you know—plow, pick, peel, put up. And we have fewer hands to do it this year. I'd rather be fishing. What about you?"

"Studying mostly. That way I can finish Miss Kate's school early and be ready for college sooner than otherwise."

"Will you be old enough?"

"Age doesn't matter as much as passing the entrance exams."

"Where are you going to college?"

Eric sighed. "My father has one idea, and I have another. We'll see." He paused. "Do you really like to fish?"

"Sure. Sam and I used to fish all the time. Mama won't let me go by myself though."

"Where did you go?"

"We have a special pond back toward the river. Biggest catfish you ever saw."

"We used to live near a lake where Father and I caught bass. Since we moved here, he has more patients and less time. I still haven't found a good spot."

Hattie pondered. She'd never fished with anyone but Sam, except when Vince tagged along. Would Mama let her go with someone else? Would she even want to?

"Maybe . . ." She took a deep breath. "Maybe I can show you our pond. I'll have to ask Mama."

Eric looked surprised, and then his face brightened.

"Uh . . . okay. That would be nice."

"All right then." She jumped up. "Have you met my dog?"

He shook his head and got up to follow her. They skirted around the dancers, hardly noticing them.

"Here, Fritter! He's learned four tricks already." She hugged the pup and rattled on and on.

"Eric, have you ever been to a shivaree? We're planning one tonight, but don't let on to Rosalie and Lester. Fritter, sit. Shivarees have to be secret in order to work. Now, shake hands with Eric, Fritter . . ."

14

Shivaree

Get out of the light, everybody," whispered Ida. "Here they come."

Hattie scooted behind the schoolhouse. Across the hard-packed dirt road, Forbes General Mercantile sat quiet and dark. A dog barked, and one shadow waved to another down the street. Soon a low rumble was heard, like distant thunder. Then the clanging of a bell shattered the quiet night, growing louder with each moment. Giggling erupted behind Hattie.

"Will you hush?" she warned. "Look . . . Here come the men."

A three-horse team thundered to a halt in front of the store. Behind them sat the gleaming, steam-powered fire engine purchased by the town only last year. Seven members of the volunteer fire brigade were aboard, one clanging the big bell with all his might. They had come to fetch the eighth member of their team—Lester.

Hattie recognized Mr. McKinney as he pounded

on the mercantile's front door. A light came on in the apartment upstairs, and Lester raised a window.

"What's all the racket?" he called down.

"We're needed at the Shelleys'!"

In the window's light Lester could be seen scratching his head. "Is this some kind of foolishness?" he shouted.

"Would we fire up this expensive contraption for foolishness?" yelled Mr. McKinney. "Hurry up, boy!"

Soon Lester appeared at the door more or less dressed. His usually slicked black hair was hanging in his eyes as he yawned. "Is it the house?" he asked.

"Don't know yet," boomed Mr. McKinney. "Let's go!"

With that, the shiny engine clanged and rumbled into the darkness. The shadows around Hattie exploded with laughter.

"They'll have a time now!" hooted Mrs. McKinney.

"Where are they taking him?" asked Lorene.

"My boys are having a party at the sawmill before they go coon hunting. They plan on losing Lester, and when he finds his way back, they'll go to the Shelleys' for a big breakfast."

"That's terrible," said Lorene.

"It's all in fun," said Ida. "Don't they have shivarees in Austin?"

"Sometimes, but I never heard of one like this."

"You're in the country now, darlin'," laughed Mrs. McKinney. "Well, shall we pay the bride a visit?"

About twenty women and girls gathered at the storefront, their hands filled with baskets and plates of food. They knocked impatiently as Rosalie appeared in her dressing gown.

"Mrs. Forbes, we heard you were all alone this evening and thought you might like some company," Ida said with a smirk on her face.

Rosalie folded her arms and gazed at the crowd of females with a funny expression. As well as Hattie knew her sister, she wasn't sure if Rosalie was aggravated, amused, or who knows what. Finally she shook her head and laughed. "I expected something, but not the fire engine!" She held open the glass door. "Come on in, ladies."

Laughing and chattering, they trooped upstairs to the newly painted three-room apartment. Boxes of belongings and gifts were stacked all around, but the presence of food and friends gave it a homey feel. Everyone ate and talked as they admired the shiny new stove, a gift from Lester's mother.

"Where is Mrs. Forbes?" asked Lorene after they had all chattered away for quite some time.

"Too tired to shivaree, I guess." Hattie stifled a yawn. "Imagine wanting to sleep when she could be here."

"Well, it's been fun, but I must turn in as well. Uncle Josef leaves early on his rounds, and this dress feels like it's been on for days."

Hattie glanced at the cool, leaf-colored dress

trimmed with narrow ivory lace. Then she stared . . . How had she missed it before?

Hanging just below Lorene's neckline on a tiny gold chain was a jeweled rose—the same pink, porcelain rose Sam had bought for a Christmas gift. In the excitement of engagement rings and underwear, Hattie had forgotten the necklace. Now it hung on Lorene, a painful reminder of an affection that could take Sam away from Hattie forever. Unless it wasn't the same one . . .

"Did Sam give you that?" she asked bluntly.

Lorene gently touched the rose and nodded. "I understand you helped him pick it out." She smiled. "It's very lovely."

Hattie shrugged and turned away. The compliment felt good. One minute it seemed like it was impossible to like this girl, and the next it was impossible not to. Would Hattie ever sort it out?

As she smothered another yawn, Mama announced it was time to go. Ida offered to stay with Rosalie until her kidnapped groom was returned.

The mantel clock struck 2 as Hattie, Mama, and Aunt Millie tiptoed into the dark house. Finding her bed full of cousins, Hattie pondered a moment, then dug a quilt out of the trunk. She spread it on the front porch and stretched out. Fritter flopped down beside her, sniffing and licking her face.

"Wondering what I'm up to, old fella?" She rubbed his silky head and tried to get comfortable on the hard cypress floor. "My bed sure would feel good right now," she mumbled, wondering what having the room to herself would be like. An empty feeling clutched her insides.

Trying to force the emptiness to leave, she listened to the cricket chorus filling the night. A bullfrog boomed in rhythm, like the bass drummer she'd heard in a band once, and owls hooted behind the barn, on the lookout for field mice. Hattie remembered the last night she'd spent outdoors, cold and alone on the river. At least this time she was at home, she thought, her eyes drooping. They opened wide as a new noise made her skin crawl.

From far away, in the swamp perhaps, came a human-like scream. It was a sound she remembered only too well. Somewhere in the night the panther prowled. She wrapped an arm around Fritter, whose nose trembled in the air.

"Don't worry, boy. It's a long way off. We'll tell Papa in the morning."

It would be unwelcome news. Since raiding the McKinney henhouse, there had been no sign of the cat, and everyone had hoped he had left the area.

Hattie tried to stop thinking about it, but she couldn't close her eyes and kept staring into the darkness. All was still except for the stars that winked high above. Papa said that folks had been looking at the same stars for thousands of years. That was comforting somehow, with life always changing. She wondered if the Lord had that in mind when He put them up there.

"Maybe Sam's watching the stars, too," she whispered to the pup.

Fritter licked her hand as if he was sure that was so. Comforted, they both fell asleep.

Though it seemed her eyes had just closed, Hattie awoke with a start. Where was she? She felt the hard floor and soft fur. Then she saw Fritter standing erect against the dark blue sky.

The sound came again, a deep, angry bellow.

"What's wrong with those cows? It's not time to milk them yet." She sat up stiffly as the noise grew louder, both cows bawling amid the thud of hooves. Fritter barked, and Hattie remembered the cry she'd heard earlier. She met Papa as he came out the door, still fastening his suspenders.

"Papa! Something's wrong with the cows, and I heard the panther last night," she said in one breath.

"What? Why didn't you tell me?"

He grabbed his gun as Uncle Burl joined them with a lantern. Together they ran into the shadows behind the barn, trying in vain to see beyond the lantern's light. Vashti's white hide flashed by ghostlike in the darkness. Hattie saw a small form bouncing beside her and was relieved that Beauty was all right.

They couldn't see Esther until rounding the blackberry patch by the old stump. She stood near the fence, bellowing into the forest. Blood streamed from cuts on her neck and face.

"Was she hung in the wire?" asked Hattie.

Papa didn't answer as he examined the cow and gently wrapped his shirt around the deepest wound.

Uncle Burl knelt by the fence with the light. "I'd say your cat's paid a visit."

Something inside Hattie went cold. She looked around desperately.

"Papa . . ." Her voice quivered despite her effort to keep it under control. "Papa, where's Esther's calf?"

Papa's face was grim. He already knew. They knelt, and in the weak light they saw tufts of rust-colored hair hanging in the bottom strand of barbed wire. Below it the ground was dark and wet. Fritter sniffed and started under the fence, but Uncle Burl grabbed the pup's collar. He pointed to paw prints and the long marks of something being dragged.

Hattie cried out and turned to bury her face in her hands.

"It's all right," said Papa, wrapping an arm around her shoulders. "At least it wasn't your little Beauty."

"But it's . . . my fault!" she sobbed. "If I'd told you . . . they'd be in the barn . . . It sounded so far off."

"It's not your fault, girl. Now that we know where to look, we'll go after the cat come sunup. You run to the house and get some medicine for Esther. She must've put up a fight."

Hattie ran toward the house. The cow's mournful lowing went straight through her. Though the male calf would have been used for meat when grown, she'd been raised to accept that. That's why she didn't play with it or even name it.

But this was different. It was still Esther's baby, and the panther was so frightening . . . Worst of all, Hattie knew she could have prevented it.

With a heavy heart, she mounted the porch stairs.

15

❖

The Panther

Two weeks had passed, with no more sign of the panther. At first what had happened hung like a shadow over the farm as Papa and Uncle Burl searched the woods all the way down to the swamp. They found tracks and what remained of the calf, but then the cat seemed to disappear—no sound, no tracks, no more raids in the night. "It's like the swamp just swallowed him up," said Papa. Hattie wished that were true.

Even so, the memory of that dark night was fading, and the sun seemed to be shining on her once again. One day she squinted as the first rays of morning spilled across the room. Now that Aunt Millie's bunch had gone, Hattie enjoyed stretching across the bed without bumping into someone.

She gazed at the wall, once covered with dress patterns. It looked pretty bare. The map Miss Kate gave her would solve that. Maybe it was time to finish and hang the sampler, too. Having your name on something made it really yours, and the room was all hers now.

Bouncing off the feather mattress, she put on a white blouse and blue skirt. Mama would fuss about her wearing them to pick peas, but they were light and cool, and the day promised to be a scorcher. Besides, she'd finish before Mama and Papa got back from town. They'd left early to buy supplies and to see Rosalie.

Hattie smiled to herself. Mama and Rosalie didn't know how to act if they couldn't talk every day. The newlyweds had already shown up several times for supper and even washed dishes. Maybe things hadn't changed as much as she thought.

"Gramma, I'm going to pick peas before it gets too hot," she called into the kitchen.

"Better tie up the pup. Your Papa won't like him stomping the vines again," said Gramma. "Don't you want to eat breakfast first?"

"When I'm through." Hattie clapped her hands. "Come here, Fritter." The black puppy bounded up the steps. "Can't he stay in with you, Gramma? He hates being tied up."

"Only if you'll eat something."

"That's a deal," said Hattie. She wolfed down a biscuit with red jelly.

"Watch for snakes, honey," said Gramma. "Your papa saw one yesterday. And don't forget your bonnet."

"Yes'm." In one motion Hattie grabbed the blue-checkered bonnet and large, white feed sack off the pegs by the door. Bounding down the steps, she went to turn out the cows first. They trotted across the pasture, Beauty romping and bucking, glad to be out after spending the night in the barn. Every creature on the place had been locked up before dark. Papa wasn't taking any more chances.

Crossing the orchard, Hattie entered the back field where two acres were lined with seemingly endless rows of peas and beans. Not long ago they had been a pretty sight in the morning. The dew-sparkled leaves with their small lavender blossoms had looked like diamonds and amethysts sprinkled about on a green cushion.

But May had been dry, and now the east Texas summer had set in unmercifully hot. The ground had baked hard, and now the brittle pea vines snapped and crackled as she waded into them. Hattie wondered where they found enough moisture to fill out.

She sighed and hoisted the wide strap sewn to the feed sack across her shoulder. The leathery, violet pods popped softly as she pulled them from the dry stalks. The bonnet flopped in her face, and she carelessly shoved it back. Why worry about a few freckles? Perfect complexions were for girls who only cared what boys thought.

Thank goodness Eric wasn't concerned about all that. He seemed more interested in fishing. After speaking to Mama, they had planned a trip to the pond next week. She could hardly wait.

Hattie worked her way down the row, stopping only now and then to wipe the sweat trickling down her cheeks. She wondered if Colorado was cooler. Soon Sam would be in Wyoming, and then it would only be weeks until the herd was delivered in Montana. There the men and horses would rest before starting the long trip back. She hoped Sam and Vince would ride the train part of the way, which would bring them home in October . . .

Her thoughts were interrupted by a strange sound . . . A growl?

Hattie stiffened, and her arms broke out in goose bumps. She looked across the field toward the pines that bordered it. Only a pair of blue jays fluttered there. Maybe her brain was baking. Varmints rarely came out of the woods in the daytime. She pulled the bonnet back on.

Then she heard it again—a human-like scream— unmistakable, blood-chilling, and so close . . . The panther!

She looked around wildly. Perhaps only fifty yards away a shadow moved in the vines.

Fear gripped Hattie. Her mind screamed to her to run, but her feet seemed frozen to the spot. "Lord, show me what to do," she whispered.

Then the shadow blended into light and took a dreadful shape. "*Please* show me what to do . . . now."

She shook her head, trying to clear it. Cats love

to chase things, and if she did run he'd catch her in a minute. Nor was there any use in calling Gramma. Even if she heard, what could she do?

Maybe the panther was just trailing a rabbit. If Hattie held perfectly still, he might move on. She clutched her skirt as the breeze gently poufed it toward the cat—he was downwind!

She held her breath and prayed as the panther stretched his massive head to taste the air. Moments that felt as long as eternity passed. Black ears twitched, and yellow eyes turned Hattie's way.

Panic seized her as she turned to flee, still clutching her sack. She ran a few strides before glancing back to see if the cat was following. It was leaping easily over the rows of peas and beans.

Hattie's foot got caught in a vine, and she went down hard, spilling the peas she'd gathered. Leaving them behind, she scrambled forward, determined not to look back again.

After just a few more steps, a horrible scream seemed to reach out for her. Hattie covered her ears and, against her will, screamed too. Irresistibly drawn, she looked back.

The beast was attacking her sack!

She choked back a sob and plunged on. Her shoes felt like lead weights, and the house seemed much too far away. Time was what she needed. Just a little more time . . .

Suddenly an idea came to her. As hard as it was,

she slowed down. She'd be less likely to trip that way and wouldn't attract as much attention.

The cat finished tearing the sack to white ribbons before noticing Hattie again. He growled, then trotted on.

Hattie was ready this time and dropped the bonnet. She walked on steadily, clenching her teeth so hard she tasted blood—anything to keep from crying or screaming or doing any of the other things she desperately wanted to do but that she knew would increase her danger.

From behind her came another squall. She looked back to see great claws ripping at the blue gingham bonnet. Hurrying on, she noticed the cows. They had heard the cat and were running wildly around. What if the beast followed her to the barn?

Nearing the edge of the field, she glanced back again. The bonnet was shredded beyond recognition. What else did she have to distract him?

Hattie looked down—the skirt would have to do. The button popped as she yanked the skirt off, thinking how Mama would say she was so hard on clothes. But Hattie was sure that in this case Mama would understand.

Hattie could hear Fritter barking wildly inside the house. His sharp ears had told him what Gramma couldn't know.

A few more steps and Hattie was out of the peas. She looked back as the cat pounced on the blue ruffled skirt. He screamed, tearing it with razor-sharp claws. Needing no further encouragement, Hattie raced around the barn. The front porch had never looked better.

Her feet barely touched the steps as Gramma opened the door.

"Girl, what in the world? Where's your skirt?"

"No! Don't let him out!" she cried, but it was too late.

A bolt of black lightning flashed through the door and across the yard. Hattie leaped, grabbing at the burly pup but only managed to grab a little fur.

"Fritter, come back!" she screamed, running after him.

Rounding the barn, she stopped in horror. Both dog and panther stood frozen in mid-stride. The cat's lips were drawn back over the gleaming fangs that looked even bigger than Hattie remembered. The red mouth hissed, and every hair on Hattie's head tried to stand on end.

Fritter looked the same way himself. From several feet away Hattie could see he was trembling. But the brave pup didn't move, and from deep within came a rumbling growl.

Why doesn't he run? Why doesn't he just turn tail and run like he did in the cow pen?

Listening to the cows going crazy, Hattie wondered what would happen if she called Fritter back. Would the cat come after them or the cows? She had to do *something*.

Desperately she looked around. A pitchfork

stood propped against the barn. She edged toward it, murmuring softly, "Fritter . . . come on, boy. Go in the house . . ."

The panther screamed and crouched lower, apparently ready to leap. Fritter jumped back a step and barked wildly.

"No, Fritter! Leave him alone!" cried Hattie.

As if propelled by giant springs, the cat leapt through the air. It landed on the pup, burying razor claws in his shoulder. Fritter shrieked painfully as they tumbled in a frightening ball of flaming eyes, white teeth, and black fur.

Seizing the pitchfork, Hattie drew near, screaming at them to stop. She knew Fritter wouldn't survive this for long. He was big and strong but too young to face an enemy like this. All she needed was a second, a break in the fight . . .

Instead the cat got a grip on Fritter's neck. In a moment, it would be over.

"Please, God, please help us!" she cried.

With a quick step forward, Hattie jabbed sharp prongs into the panther's side. He rolled away with a scream that sliced through her like a hot knife.

She didn't know how long he faced her, crouched and ready to spring, blood trickling down his side. She could only stand transfixed by the fiery, yellow eyes and dripping fangs.

Fritter moaned. From the corner of her eye, Hattie saw him try to rise and then sink back. She moved slowly, trying to get between him and the cat.

The beast hissed and crouched even lower. Hattie wondered if she even stood a chance with a pitchfork.

"Go on, you . . .you . . ." She hissed back, anger almost overcoming her fear. This terrible beast had killed their calf, and now maybe Fritter . . .

Once again the powerful haunches unleashed as the cat leaped straight for Hattie. Clutching the pitchfork, she braced it against her thigh and closed her eyes.

The force of the heavy body drove her to the ground, the handle torn from her hands. The panther's screams tore the air. She wrapped her arms around her head, afraid of what was about to happen but helpless to stop it.

She heard a loud crack—followed by silence.

"Honey, are you all right?"

With great effort, Hattie opened her eyes. She saw Gramma, her face twisted with pain and worry. Gramma limped across the yard, using Papa's heavy rifle as a crutch.

How had she managed it? Hattie wanted to ask but found that she couldn't speak.

Fritter whimpered and raised his head. Hattie tried to stand, but her knees felt like butter. The panther lay motionless between them, his face twisted in a terrible snarl.

She crawled around to Fritter and stroked him with trembling hands. The seriously wounded pup whined as Gramma examined him. His neck was covered with blood, and his shoulder was cut so deep she could see the bone. A huge sob choked Hattie.

"Now, now . . ." said Gramma, holding Hattie's head on her shoulder and rocking her, just like when Hattie was a young child.

"How bad is he, Gramma?"

"Not as bad as it looks. It didn't get his windpipe, and we can sew this shoulder right up. First we'll need some water and clean sheets. Can you get them?"

Hattie nodded and leaned over to hug Fritter. He stopped whining and licked her salty face. Then slowly she tested her wobbly knees.

"There now," said Gramma with a tender smile. "You're a brave pair of young'uns, and you'll both be fine. God was watching over us today, and He helped us both do more than we could."

Hattie nodded and started for the house, her legs growing steadier. The morning mist had cleared, leaving a brilliant blue sky over the piney woods. Looking up, she squeezed herself a little.

"Thanks, Father, for being with us . . . no matter what."

She turned back to call out, "Gramma! Wait'll Sam hears about this!"